Praise for *Única Looking at the Sea*

This is a novel that questions and p~   to
compel us to see, beyond the limits ~
we truly are in our garbage, ir

You have to read it ar
the human condition, alw.
and the sublime. It is a novel
and perhaps brings us, like Únic
last reflection of a possible hope.

⌐oject
⌐iallenges us
~ with the sea, the

—*Mabel Morvillo*

Única Looking at the Sea, the first novel by the Costa Rican writer Fernando Contreras Castro, has immediately assumed a position of great importance in the history of Costa Rican literature. Beginning with a space—the problematic and deeply referential space of the sanitary landfill at Río Azul—this work goes beyond the anecdotal to acquire the symbolic character and the critical capacity of great literary work. We can say that through this writer's ingenuity garbage is turned into literature, with the garbage dump serving as the basis for an incisive critique of modern consumer culture.

From within this grotesque, almost nonsensical, realism, moments of immense tenderness emerge, of solidarity and of human suffering. The subtle irony and sometimes cruel sarcasm recreate one of the cruelest realities in our society.

—*Amalia Chaverri*

This is a story so truthful, so sad, so real that it slips into one's soul, and we suffer with the characters, suffer their troubles, their pain and the grief of those lives that have been discarded and found themselves in this garbage dump called Río Azul (what a pretty name for a residential neighborhood!).

This book should touch the conscience of many Costa Ricans unaware of these social realities that are very close to all of us but disregarded in our indifference and our egotism.

—*Luisa González*

Única Looking at the Sea is a great achievement for its creative brilliance and for its relevance to our world, and because it succeeds in awakening in the reader the vision of what garbage signifies for those two opposing social groups: those who produce it and throw it out, and those who collect it and survive thanks to it. Foul-smelling reality.

—*Maritza Castro*

Única Looking at the Sea, the first novel by Fernando Contreras Castro, tells the story of a discarded family, a family of "divers" in 1992. It contrasts the rich and the powerful— the actual President, the presidential offices of Zapote, the families of the richest neighborhoods—with the most despised and the poorest—Río Azul and its divers—, and in that discarded family there develops one of the most tender and terrible love stories I have ever read: The story of love that a woman already advanced in years, Única Oconitrillo, professes for her adoptive son, Bacán, a little boy found in the dump, and between Única and Momboñombo Moña Gallo, a man that, tired of an unlivable life, decides one day "to throw himself into the garbage."

—*Anacristina Rossi*

Diálogos

ÚNICA LOOKING AT THE SEA

ÚNICA MIRANDO AL MAR

by

Fernando Contreras Castro

Translated by

Elaine S. Brooks

DIÁLOGOS
DIÁLOGOSBOOKS.COM

Única Looking at the Sea
by Fernando Contreras Castro
a translation of *Única mirando al mar,* Copyright © Fernando Contreras Castro.
English translation by Elaine S. Brooks.
Translation copyright © 2017 by Elaine S. Brooks and Diálogos Books.

Front cover photo by the author.

Printed in the U.S.A.
First Printing
10 9 8 7 6 5 4 3 2 1 17 18 19 20 21 22

Library of Congress Control Number: 2017948584
Contreras Castro, Fernando
Única Looking at the Sea / Fernando Contreras Castro
with Elaine S. Brooks (translator)
p. cm.

ISBN: 978-1-944884-29-1 (pbk.)
978-1-944884-30-7 (ebook)

DIÁLOGOS
AN IMPRINT OF LAVENDER INK
DIÁLOGOSBOOKS.COM

Translator's Acknowledgments

San Ramón, Costa Rica has been my summer home for many years while I taught on the University of New Orleans-Costa Rica Summer Program. When preparing a course on ecological issues in Costa Rican literature, I began reading Fernando Contreras Castro's novels and I was immediately attracted to the novel *Única mirando al mar;* the novel that gives a voice to the voiceless, to the fictional characters representative of all those who live in grinding poverty. The main character, Única, shares her resilient strength and her struggle to maintain a dignified order to her household with her mentally challenged son, Bacán, and the man who would become her husband, Mondolfo Moya Garro (Momboñombo). The novel takes place on a landfill outside of San José, Costa Rica where Única, her family, and a multitud of divers from all walks of life strive to earn a living. Contreras Castro's narrative realistically portrays characters that are intrinsically woven into the vivid descriptions of the dump's toxic living conditions. Translating the depth of emotions, Única's hope, Mondolfo's despair, and every shade of emotional nuance to tell the story of the divers' daily toil in the dump's muck and quicksand was a challenge and a joy.

No creative work comes to fruition without the help of editing and multiple readers. I am grateful to Lisbeth Philip for the late night editing sessions in which we read aloud every word in English and Spanish. I also want to acknowledge Silvia Gómez Juarez. I would like to thank don Óscar Montanaro for encouraging me to take on this project, and Marie Kaposchyn for her friendship during the many years that she and I have worked and travelled in Costa Rica. I am blessed to have made many friends in Costa Rica, with special reference to Patrycia Ramírez Salas and Roberto Céspedes Porras. Thank you for your encouragement, your help with the editing, your friendship, and the wonderful times we have shared together. To Bill Lavender, Editor-in-Chief of Diálogos, I give you many thanks for your patience and for your expertise during the process of publication.

And many thanks to Fernando Contreras Castro, who continues to craft novels that inspire me and compel me to see the invisible suffering of marginalized people.

Elaine S. Brooks

Preface to the 21st Anniversary Edition

Celebrating twenty-one years appeals to me more than celebrating the time-honored twentieth year. I prefer odd numbers. Twenty-one like the Major Arcana Tarot cards, which begin with the Fool and end with the World.

Twenty years is nothing, but one cannot say that about twenty-one.

In 1993 I published one thousand copies in a private edition of a brief novel that I had been writing for some months. It all started from one single image: a man of a mature age loses everything and decides to throw himself away. He literally throws himself into the trash, allowing a garbage truck to take him to the city's largest dump, perhaps with the intention of letting himself die. Once he is in the dump he gets involved with the underworld of the so-called divers, rejected people, without any other place on Earth.

From this image I tried to recreate the daily life of people who live off what the rest of society throws away without ever imagining that all that trash becomes the last possibility that a system based on injustice offers them.

The novel made its own path. Like the Arcana Zero, the Fool, it set off with no more resources than a few images in its bundle. In the course of these twenty-one years, its characters have told their stories in high school and university classrooms, from town to town, in my language and in foreign languages.

Independently of the author's expectations, the novel has created its own story, its own life.

To mark the ten years since its publication, what began as proofreading ended with a complete rewriting of the text. The two versions have coexisted since that time generating more than a few controversies about whether or not the writer has the right to rewrite a book that the reading public had made theirs. The version that the reader now has in hand is the most recent, the one with which the writer finally feels satisfied.

The novel will continue its course from hand to hand, from eye to eye, from tooth to tooth. The reader will always have the last word. The book will depend on the reader's wishes as to whether it continues going forward. This edition will appear like a train station where it will get off from the train that brought it, board a new one and continue rolling while finding readers and travellers who will make a place for it in their backpack. The writer is grateful to each person who lends a hand, an eye, or a tooth to this unrepentant wanderer; and to whoever offers it shelter with no other commitment than to speak with the book the entire night, knowing that at dawn it will inexorably continue its journey.

Fernando Contreras Castro
San José, October 21, 2014

Preliminary Remarks

"When writing a novel, this author is not interested in situations or people from reality except to assess through them the true reality of people and situations. That is why the former are not the ones that take shape in the story. Do not look for this book's characters in your memory. Find them in your heart and in the comparison of many lives and some incidents that you may remember, within your own life and conscience."

The previous paragraph, a foreword written by me for one of my novels—that perhaps some readers fail to digest in practice due to their lack of imagination that prevents them from making the literary creative act independent of a more fundamental dissemination of ideas, of simple facts or temporary situations that the act seems to include—could also have been written for *Única Looking at the Sea*, albeit the author may have ascribed to the literary act and its concrete circumstances of time and space perhaps a greater presence of the strictly indispensable as the seed for his work.

Because the value of the story told here, an original work and the catalyst of so many possible implications that exceed any measure in gold and is miles away from the fleeting circumstances of its locale, resides in its being a literary act supreme in its imaginative beginning and its play on sharp contrasts between humans and society that the author has put adrift to blossom in an ocean of urban debris. The then and now monstrous *trash heap*, reeking and present still, transformed by the author with his magic wand into another very distinct reality; into a character from a categorically different world, built on abstractionism and the profound grand metaphor from where, as from the foul-smelling swamp from which the lotus flowers spring forth so proverbially human-like in idiomatic figures of speech, his characters begin to rise, to toss and turn and live as beloved creatures from his creation. They are the charismatic and humanistic marionettes, horribly beautiful called: Única –a wild lily-, teacher and mother until she looks at her sea, which is death; Momboñombo her Resurrected Man, who bursts upon that underworld, a poet himself without knowing it, changed into a miracle cure, even a revolutionary one due to the loving matriarch's influence; Bacán, Única´s son by her own maternal and divine decree, her hopelessly eternal child to the limits of life and death; and the parody of a priest or a pastor, or better still a priest and a pastor unlike the usual pastors because he becomes one by his own consecration and ludic whim. He is the one whom the novelist has named Oso Carmuco and has dressed in cardinal red- we do not know if this is supposed to turn us red with laughter, or with shame based on what his ingenuous and lonely ministry contains and signifies; and many more minor characters that along with the others the reader will come to know at times between sobs and at other times between the irresistible urge to burst out laughing. It is the transformation of the surrounding trash into the human spirit thanks to the passionate ability of a keen talent poured into an intelligent fictional storyline that enriches the nation's narrative and constitutes an example that is at the same time tender and strong, hard and kind, painful and comical and from which can be written realities that are popular and very much our own in Costa Rican Spanish, although its human potential makes the work universally real and moving.

Such is the case of Fernando Contreras Castro and his outstanding cunning and brutal joke that is equally a tender and joyful love story with an intense and final poetic resonance.

Fabián Dobles

Preface to the English Edition

In 1992 on a day like any other, I began to write the first version of *Única Mirando al Mar (Única Looking at the Sea)*. On another day like any other in 1993, the novel was published. Years later I decided to rewrite it. The second version forever substituted the first version. On both occasions I was fully conscious that I was writing on the topic of marginality in which thousands of people live around the world, searching for their sustenance in waste and garbage.

25 years have gone by until this day like any other in 2017 in which this new edition appears from the second and definitive version of the novel.

Now as one more reader of the text (at best, as its author, given that among my few convictions is that one is only a writer when one is seated writing), I believe that the validity of this story rests on the fact that neither the landscape it depicts, nor the characters it narrates are on the fringe, but to the contrary, they are people perfectly inserted into the boundaries of a predatory system that could not sustain itself except on the platform of social injustice; a system that needs to produce as much material garbage as human garbage so that in a handful of privileged people its promise may be fulfilled even at the inestimable price of the final destruction of the planet.

Única Looking at the Sea was born like a bleeding

wound that will never cease calling attention to this point. The kind readers who reach the end of the novel will understand that what was unusual was not the names of the characters but rather their brief, absurd and incomparable lives spent doing the unpleasant labor of surviving from everyone else's trash.

Fernando Contreras Castro
On a day like any other in 2017, San José

Única Looking at the Sea

For my grandparents
Rafael Castro Piepper and
Amparo Villegas de Castro
In memoriam

…Celso Coropa recogió en la palma de su mano un rayo de sol y suspiró: -¡Hay veces en que no me gusta la vida!... Frente a él había como una tortura de raíces y bejucos. ¡...Y hay veces que sí!—añadió. Entre la tortura de raíces y bejucos había una flor.

...Celso Coropa picked up a ray of sun in his palm and sighed: There are times when I do not like life! In front of him there was a torture of roots and vines. And there are times, he added, when between the torture of roots and vines there is a flower.

Carlos Salazar Herrera
La montaña

More from long habit than any other principle of order in the world, the sun began to rise, hesitating along the edge of the hill, as if at the last minute it had decided to light one more day instead of rushing into the abyss of the previous night.

All quiet on the Western front, the flies were yawning and the buzzards were shaking the early morning leftovers from their wings.

In the persistent drizzle and the toxic vapors from that unchanging sea, the night divers took a tally of the cargo extracted from the depths. Before the day divers arrived to add their arm strokes, the night divers hustled to sort out from their haul the edible and the sellable items. The second category included aluminum cans, glass bottles, all types of paper and other metals, for which the smelters scarcely paid more.

The day divers were just beginning to awaken, still stretching and yawning when they opened the doors to their makeshift shacks on the shantytown's beaches bursting from the sea of plastic fish.

Those who were coming from afar readied themselves once again to ascend the fossilized clay hill that led to the last stop of the city's bad conscience.

Around six o'clock in the morning, two enormous tractors were also prodded awake by hunger. With their tyrannosaurus jaws open, they could hardly wait for the tons of waste the city would send them day after day.

With patience learned from routine, their operators ate the usual breakfast of coffee with milk and a sweet roll before getting into the machines and starting the rigorous job of piling up, turning over and placing from side to side, like an artificial tide, the constant influx of trash that would arrive relentlessly in the garbage trucks.

At eight o'clock in the morning the sun was already precariously illuminating the mortal remains of that October drowned by so much rain.

From faraway one could see the hill that supported the garbage dump with its insides torn apart under the open sky, like an ant hill of women, men and children of indecipherable ages, rats and mice, dogs and buzzards, and hundreds of thousands of insects, all indistinguishable in the rumination that the city had given up as unusable, searching for what chance might also have cast aside; all in an ebb and flow of trash from the constant movement of the tractors.

No one among the members of the more than two hundred families, who at that time earned their livelihood in Río Azul, could offer information as to whether or not there had ever been a river in that place; even less if that river, supposing it had run through there, had been blue. Anyway, there remained only the sea tides kicked up by the two tractors that accommodated from dawn to dawn, the tons of trash that the city would send in ever more generous amounts.

At the bottom of the hill, the neighboring

communities attempted in vain to protect themselves from the trash with a wire fence.

A gate restricted access. At the entrance an attendant kept watch from the guardhouse where he checked the drivers' permits before allowing them to enter with their disagreeable load.

The neighborhood school also adjoined the wire fence.

A foul stench overpowered the sticky atmosphere that was inhaled in Río Azul's environment: it was the stench of the soup of all the rancid broth from tons of crushed trash, the broth that spilled over and ran down like a river of poison between the cracks of the ulcerated land's body.

That lethal river must have been born, like other rivers are usually born, from a small stream, having grown, and having poured out into the sea. But in this case, the river's birth, growth and death occurred in the same place, and its corpse was being filtered toward the subsoil's water tables.

On the surface above, the divers knew nothing about the malignant masses that were growing under their feet. For years they had clomped on that quicksand and they had grown accustomed to the carpet of waste that extended unmercifully, covering everything.

Day by day the divers would gather at the most unpredictable hours to sift through the trash, like always, like before, when it would arrive in pick-up trucks and in enormous drums; like afterwards, when it began to travel in first class, in specialized collectors that opened their bowels and devoured the sacks of waste by means of a complex hydraulic mechanism.

The divers yearned for the traditional transport, almost in disuse, because in the pick-up trucks things were not so mistreated; the bottles would not break, nor the still useful artifacts that fate, not the intention of people, would throw away undistinguishable in amongst the trash.

In the dump's early years, the garbage was more of an organic type. Food leftovers and fruit peels would arrive. The rest was divided between glass, aluminum, and wood from old beaten up furniture that in the dump would be appreciated again because it either became the shantytown's furnishings or firewood for the homes.

The aluminum cans and the glass bottles were sold. If a can made of zinc arrived, it was used to reinforce a wall or part of a roof, even if it was rusty. Of course nobody expected someone to throw out a can in good shape.

With those materials that were second-hand, third-hand and even more hands, Única Oconitrillo had rebuilt the meaning of her life. She had sworn that she would be taken directly from the classroom to the cemetery. Once she landed in the dump, she learned not to swear.

Several founders of the divers' community welcomed the teacher and helped her to put up her shack, at times even with pieces generously donated from neighboring shacks. Única, who was an unshakable optimist, felt happy and safe in her new home.

"There's nothing here, but you can find everything."

"It could be worse."

"Don't exaggerate doña Única."

"I don't exaggerate!"

"Doña Única, the first night is always the worst. If you need anything, call us."

"Thank you!"

"There are good people everywhere," thought Única Oconitrillo that first night between borrowed blankets, but on her own pieces of cardboard. She did not feel alone. She slept. She awoke two and a half hours later, rolled one end of her blanket, bit down on it forcefully and cried until dawn.

As she was a recent arrival, at first light the teacher Oconitrillo looked for water to wash her face and hands. As she was a recent arrival, she learned that if she wanted water she would have to go down the hill with a bucket, ask for it from some neighbor and carry it back to her house.

What they did not tell her was that it was becoming more and more difficult to convince the neighbors that the divers asked for water because no water pipe went up to the top of the hill, as it had never been planned as a place where human life would toil.

A short time after the first inhabitants settled on the dump's hill, the neighbors suspected the problem that the settlers would become over the years. So, they decided to cut off humanitarian aid to convince them at the very least to leave at the end of the day and return in the morning, as you would expect of any daytime job.

"Truly there are good people everywhere," Única would repeat trudging uphill with her face clean and her bucket full.

Única Oconitrillo numbered her apron along with her very few belongings. She wrapped it around her, breathed deeply and went out to join her neighbors who had already been diving for almost an hour. By the middle of the morning she had already filled two shopping bags.

"None of that is of any use, doña Única. You have to look for what you can eat or what you can sell."

In that moment her happiness vanished, and in that moment her last bit of innocence was torn to shreds when she understood that the phrase "living off trash" was not metaphorical, but rather the awful truth.

"Don't cry, Miss Única. At first it's very hard, but later on everyone gets used to it."

"But doesn't it disgust you?"

"It is disgusting not to eat."

Then her mood lifted: Única studied each one of their faces, don Conce and don Retana, already so elderly, and so determined to live that they could snatch bread from the tractor's scoop loader. She was looking from face to face, like a butterfly over shriveled flowers, but in each face she found approval. At the end of the long line, Única Oconitrillo was convinced that they had revealed a truth to her: "It is disgusting not to eat." Never again would she grimace at her daily bread, although not even for that reason would her heart abandon the feeling that a garbage dump was not a place for human beings. She was just about to say it, but it became impossible in that moment to translate that certainty, which she would carry between her chest and her back while she still had a chest and a back into which her heart would fit.

Toward nightfall, Única summoned her neighbors, spoke to them about brotherly love and instituted the custom of dining together, on the condition that each one would contribute something to the common pot.

"She's a teacher..."

"Maybe she's right."

The shantytown was at that time a "new neighborhood." Migrants from the countryside and other dispossessed people had formed the community of divers who had faithfully followed the dump from its two previous dwelling places where the neighbors, having grown weary of it, succeeded in getting rid of it after five years and seven years respectfully, according to the legend. But a long life awaited Río Azul as the location for what had never taken place in any other part of the world.

Don Retana, the one who lived in the shack farthest away, was a retired sailor, an old man but still strong, with all the ailments of those who spend their life on a ship. Among them, the most painful of all was his yearning for the sea. The old man would speak even when alone. While he was diving shoulder to shoulder with the younger people, he would take the opportunity to tell infinite stories.

"Often he loses it. He acts dumb with his mouth hanging open, and at other times he starts speaking in English that he says he learned with the sailors from other countries."

Don Concepción was a sickly old man who arrived from the banana plantation zone.

"He was already screwed up. He came because they had fired him for being old."

"They say that when he arrived, he couldn't find even one family member living in the city."

"He's fucked to the bone. Sometimes he needs help getting up because he falls down and he can't do it alone."

From those souls of every kind of character, Única learned to distinguish the edible from the recyclable, and she added a few categories that for the other divers were of no importance; like the one that classified the bits of leftover soap for washing the plates from her dinnerware, and toothbrushes for everyone, even though nobody but she would use them; another for the small bottles of perfume to wear on Sundays when going down to hear Mass; another for combs and hair adornments and things of that sort which put together were scarcely enough to repair the broken down scaffolding of her illusions each time she felt them diminishing.

On the first Sunday of the fifth month after settling into her life at the dump, Única lost her last innocence when the priest at the church wouldn't let her go to Mass. He asked her not to come back until she found work and could appear decently in the house of God. And not even then, because she had left a stench in the pew where she had been sitting.

"God does not despise any of his creatures."

"God reigns in heaven, but I am in charge here, and I don't want the church to fill up with vagrants."

"That son of a bitch!" grumbled don Conce, but Única asked him not to use swear words.

On Sundays the garbage trucks would not arrive to deposit their daily bread. That day was also an obligatory rest for the tractors because their operators did not see them again until Monday.

For Única that Sunday was the first one in her life she could recall without a seven o'clock Mass. The entire morning the feeling of having offended the priest weighed heavily on her like a curse. But no matter how often she replayed the scene in her mind, she could find no motive of any kind for having been treated in that way.

"As if I were trash!" she said aloud. When she heard herself utter that injustice, a hideous clarity engulfed her soul:

"Of course, they see us as if we were trash."

Humiliation turned her eyes into a sea of salty hot tears that forced her to submerge her face into the bucket of water. She did not allow herself to drown right there and then because she had already chosen life.

"That son of a bitch!"

That was how she used the first curse word in her life, and she was consoled only by the conviction that whatever that soulless man might say, neither he nor anyone else would convince her that God would look unfavorably upon her just because life had cornered her on that hill together with the rest of the scraps.

She didn't return to the church, but, like a miracle that supported her conviction, she assumed ownership of the unusual discovery of a rosary made of plastic beads that arrived with other costume jewelry, wrapped apart in a handkerchief knotted at the ends. From that time on, for Holy Week, Única led the Friday evening rosary for the resident divers, until the day young Carmen arrived with the story that he had become a priest. Everyone was astonished to see him dressed in purple with a cassock over his rags.

"I found it in the first bag I opened."

His name was Carmen and he walked like a bear. That's why they called him Oso Carmuco. He must have been around twenty years old at that time and his sharp features helped to establish his appearance as a mystic, which he needed in order to convince the rest of the people. Although convincing them, after all, was not too complicated. Perhaps because nobody had so much time as to sit down and discuss the motives of his conversion. After the explosion of laughter, it seemed like a good idea to everyone…

"We needed a priest here in the dump."

"And it's even better if he's from here because in that way there's more trust."

"And since he works the same way we do, he's not going to go off on us with that nonsense that we smell bad."

"God knows what he is doing," said Única, and she delivered the rosary into the hands of the young man. Afterwards, during periods of rest, little by little she began to teach him what he should say with each decade of beads.

It was tremendously difficult for Carmen to memorize the subject matter of the five Mysteries, the fifty Hail Mary's with an Our Father before each one, and another at the end, before three more Hail Mary's and a Salve, followed by litanies that were more difficult because they did not have beads on the rosary. It was a mess that almost finished off his ministry. All the more so in that Única obliged him to repeat, until he was exhausted, an infinite number of prayers that he confused and pronounced as a jumble of mishmash in the middle, which luckily for him nobody but a few ladies noticed and they turned a blind eye.

"Don't miss Oso Carmuco's Mass! You'll die of laughter."

"But if you laugh, doña Única will scold you."

"Yes, but no one pays attention to her."

The agreement was that during the workweek Carmen would be a diver as he had always been, but on Sundays, dressed in the cassock and with the rosary in his hand, he would be the dump's priest. This deal suited him very well, overall because he was not ready to give up carousing with his friends, nor the nocturnal adventures in the city's neighborhoods of ill repute.

"As long as he doesn't do it when he's officiating, there's no problem."

"Everyone already knows that's how men are. What the hell!"

* * *

Not too far from the diving zones, Bacán, who may have been five or six years old, was waiting while seated on the back of a stove with four heating coils that had run aground there long ago, as evidenced by the stickiness on the shell of its prow. The child liked to sit there because his unique position gave him a panoramic view of the place. From there he watched the hustle and bustle of the divers, the arrival and the departure of the garbage trucks, the flight of the buzzards, the clouds of flies and the sea of trash. Seated there he played with whatever he could; usually with toys tossed away that the adults rescued for him from the jaws of the tractors.

Something gleamed for an instant from the blackness of the garbage. The child got down from his stove and advanced a little into the trash. The glow of the light became confused among thousands of fleeting sparkling lights, which forced Bacán to go back over his steps in order to attempt a new search. The twinkling glow and his curiosity led him to an object half buried in the garbage. He took hold of it where he could and he pulled with all his strength. Something almost round came out and it began to resemble a golden apple as he was rubbing it against his tee shirt. It was a golden apple with an inscription that after much effort he managed to read:

"FFFoooor ththe mmmmmooost beeeeuttifffuul gggirrrl…" "For the most beautiful girl."

Bacán hid the apple under his tee shirt and returned to his spot. Once he was seated comfortably, he spent a couple of hours repeating aloud the enigmatic phrase until he gave up on his attempt to understand it. A little weary, he stood up balancing himself carefully on his skinny legs, he planted his feet as squarely as he could and threw the apple in the direction of where it had come out. As if inhaled by a yawning earth, the apple sank forever with its frustrating message.

Única observed the scene from afar. With a frantic look she left the diving zone to run to the place where she thought she had seen the golden object fall; but neither her best effort, nor her vast experience in deep sea diving helped her to recover the thing. She turned her face toward the child and looked at him with her brows and her lips arched, as if that insignificant act had drawn on her countenance an arc of despair:

"Bacancito, what was that?"

Bacán reciprocated the gesture and added to it a shrug of his shoulders, which made it clear to the woman that even pulling time back by its roots, she would not be able to find out what that thing was that the child had scorned without judgment.

Like so many things of inestimable value, Única had found the child in the trash almost four years ago. The little one had been playing absent-mindedly as if it had not mattered to him that he was alone. She attracted his attention and he held out his arms to her. The hug sealed the alliance between them. After a few weeks of asking around, the woman assumed that the child was as alone in the world as she, and there was no more doubt on that subject. From then on Bacán was her child and she was his mother.

Raising a child in Río Azul's garbage dump was never easy. But it would have been a difficult task for Única Oconitrillo to tolerate the twenty years she had spent as a diver without that little boy whom she had found in the trash when he could do no more than repeat the only word he knew: "bacán," to which he owed his name.

Reading material would come to the dump: books and newspapers that Única used to teach Bacán to read. He was the only child among the neighborhood children who attended lessons in spite of the constant taunting by the rest of the residents for whom learning such a thing brought no benefits at all. Única justified her efforts with an educator's consistent arguments:

"In this country education is free and mandatory, and one has to take it seriously..." In the community everyone was already accustomed to the good lady's crazy ideas.

When he reached six or seven years old, because his age might never be known, the woman had already taught the boy something about reading, as one might expect from a lady who in her better years had been a teacher. Of course, a teacher's aide, that is to say, without a degree or formal education. She was one of those recruited by the Department of Public Education when there was a shortage of teachers with degrees. It was work that doña Única Oconitrillo practiced with tenacity from sixteen years of age to almost thirty, until she was let go when the shortage of professionals was over. It was a period that coincided, because misfortunes never arrive alone, she would repeat, with the death of her mother and her entry into the lines of human outcasts. All of this had happened, "and to top it off," she would repeat, "in October, in full hurricane season," by which her life was counted from October to October, almost from nothing to nothing, if not for her stubborn faith that her situation was not going to last forever and that even an irremediable thing had a remedy if one put a good face on it.

Bacán was around twenty-five, plus or minus a few years, and Única was about fifty or so years old, not because she did not want to reveal her age, but rather because she had lost count. Twenty years of watching her child grow up, and both of them watching the unstoppable growth of the dump; and in the dump, being a part of the shantytown's growth, to which new neighbors never stopped coming to build new shacks with whatever old material happened to end up there. With her irrepressible optimism, Única had given that "neighborhood" the name of "Barrio Las Rosas," due to a white rose bush she planted when she first arrived and which had not taken root, not even at the beginning when the trash did not arrive by the tons and when throughout the area there was a current of fresh air, and the land had not been poisoned with the lethal broth from the waste.

Of the white rose bush there remained only a nice memory of what it had not become; of the fresh air there did not remain even a pleasant memory, and of the healthy land, only a hard crust in summer and a slippery terrain during the rainy season.

In twenty years the hill irremediably ended up converted into a trash dump. As the demand for space increased, the administration had more and more trees chopped down, until only an inhospitable cone remained of the hill from where the birds had fled. In twenty years, the town of Río Azul saw itself reduced to the compulsory route of the garbage trucks and everything, the houses, the church, and the school took on the color of dust that swirled down from the summit of waste.

Of the good neighbors from the very beginning, some survived. The rest were people who had degenerated, friendly at times, aggressive at times, according to whether or not they had something in their stomachs. Única would say, "How are they *not* going to be like that!"

* * *

The light of a midafternoon like so many others filtered between the scarce eyelashes of an old man. Between flashes of light, remnants from his nightmare and his bewilderment, the old man tried to direct his attention toward something that was moving in front of his eyes. After a long while, he managed to focus better and he saw a woman fanning him with a piece of cardboard, and a boy giving him shade with his skinny body, keeping him free from the horde of flies that were fighting for him in the middle of their desperate buzzing.

Única and Bacán had stumbled upon the man lying unconscious in the trash and they had dedicated half the morning to the arduous task of resurrecting him. When the man finally opened his eyes, she addressed her first words to him:

"How do you do, Única Oconitrillo, at your service."

The man sat up sluggishly and looked first at the woman, then at the boy. He had a look of astonishment like someone who had given himself up for dead and suddenly, without previous warning, wakes up and realizes that he has still not reached the benefits of death.

"We have been here for hours taking care of you, sir. If we hadn't, the flies and the buzzards would have already made you their lunch."

It was difficult for the man to understand the words. He was sunburned and a splitting headache was tearing his soul apart. Única asked for help. Between several people they lifted him and took him to the Oconitrillo home, where they stripped him of the few extra clothes he was wearing. With rags dipped in water on his forehead, at room temperature for lack of refrigeration, they lowered his fever and when they considered him to be out of danger, they let him sleep. And he slept long and hard as if he were attempting to bring back the death that had been ripped away from him. He slept for hours and hours between dreams and delirium.

The old man awoke toward the end of the afternoon, when the sun seemed to be at the point of submerging into that dead sea like one more piece of trash.

That night, with great effort he managed to get to the door of the shack and sat down there. He did not say anything. He did not speak to anyone and he rejected all the recycled food his unexpected savior offered him.

For Única Oconitrillo one thing was not under discussion: at seven o'clock at night, Bacán would go to bed on his cardboard and fall asleep. She made a few more rounds in her house putting away something here and there, picking up the mismatched pieces of her dinnerware brought together throughout the years. She recounted meticulously her set of silverware as varied as the rest of the collection, and when she considered everything to be in its place, around eight o'clock, eight thirty, she settled down on her cardboard and fell asleep immediately.

The presence of the man in the threshold to the entrance did not alter her routine. Única made one last attempt to get a word out of him and when she failed, she left him there contemplating how even the night was disposable and would scarcely fit in the dump.

"He must be thinking about something serious," she muttered once she was wrapped in her blanket. But the man was not thinking about anything. He endured the pain in his head without complaining so as not to be a nuisance. He was still not over the surprise of the worst day of his life, or the day following the worst, or the day that followed that one, when Única lost her patience and confronted him:

"Sir, you will tell me at least what your name is or you will leave here… This is a decent dump, and I can't have a stranger in my house if I don't even know what his name is."

The man looked into her eyes for the first time. She could not avoid a feeling of awe.

The man remembered his name. A somewhat vague smile appeared only to be extinguished immediately. What did his name mean? Had it had meaning at one time? He had already decided that it had not, but now it seemed urgent to pronounce it even if only to lengthen a little that parenthesis, the only one in his life in which someone had taken charge of him.

He remembered his name, Mondolfo Moya Garro, and he remembered the humor he caused as a child when his best effort was barely sufficient to pronounce it, "Momboñombo Moña Gallo." He let out a laugh of pity for that child, and in honor of him, he turned toward the woman and said: "Momboñombo Moña Gallo." He laughed again and he said with a kind of sarcasm, "My name is something like that!"

Única did not understand anything. The man insisted that it was his real name, and there was no more discussion. When asked what in the hell he was doing when he was found three days ago asleep in the middle of the dump, he limited himself to answer:

"Well, I threw myself into the trash because I am no longer useful for anything" and he laughed again.

Única's soul crumbled. She remained silent and looked at him for a long while. Afterwards she sighed and said, "But you look good, *good*!" and she continued looking at him sadly.

Mondolfo Moya Garro began to speak slowly.

"That day I got up early in the morning, I put everything in its place, I looked at the old photos of my family, the ones that I still had, I opened the cage for the canary, I locked the door to my house and ready or not, I threw myself into the trash. I climbed up onto the garbage truck and the men didn't even ask me anything, they just brought me here. Afterwards I don't know what happened. I think I fainted."

Única hadn't gotten over her astonishment. She was only looking at him and insisting: "But you look fine, *fine*. We can still squeeze more out of you for a good time to come!"

And she continued milling words between her false teeth until the man interrupted her to ask her if she had a cup of coffee around there that she could offer him. Única answered what she would always answer:

"Yes, there is, but it's not done yet."

Bacán had followed closely the old man's recovery. Now he was happy because he assumed that if the man had even said his name, then he was no longer going to die, like the diver had claimed into whose hands destiny had placed the salvation of the community's souls; a role he assumed with so much determination that he had already spent three days anxiously waiting with some miniature glass bottles with the logo of a famous seasoning sauce in his hand, ready to apply Extreme Unction to the recent arrival, because he insisted that, "that man is already a cadaver, Única, and what's happening is that he hasn't realized it."

Mr. Mondolfo had listened stupefied to the discussion between Única and Carmen about his vital signs, and for the first time he felt relief to be alive when he saw the man move away with the little bottles and lose himself among the sea of black seagulls. The image of that man wandering off convinced him that even God threw away in that place what was no longer of use to him.

"This is Bacán, my little boy.... say hello to the man, Bacancito…"

Don Mondolfo Moya Garro lifted his gaze to the height of the boy's face. He figured he was twenty years old, at a minimum. He was tall, very skinny, with a white complexion blackened by the sun and by the vapors from the dump, with dark green eyes, a black beard that was scraggly and matted, and a kind of dopey expression.

"Good to meet you, sir."

"Good to meet you, my son."

* * *

Toward nightfall, the nearest neighbors began to arrive at Única's house, as custom dictated.

"In the beginning we were just a handful of people, and we all knew each other and we ate together. Now there are so many people here that hardly anyone knows anyone else."

Mondolfo Moya Garro made an effort in vain to

understand the logic that ruled in that world. The divers arrived with bags of food and everything was heated on a campfire to one side of the shack to be handed out later in equal portions by Única's hand of Solomon.

When his plate arrived, Mondolfo wished he had never been born.

"It is disgusting not to eat!" proclaimed the matriarch wisely, before the newly arrived man had time to say something impolite.

"Nice to meet you, Momboñombo Moña Gallo, at your service." Few people looked up at him.

Única handed out the silverware and she picked it up devoutly after dinner.

Mr. Mondolfo could not eat a bite as much as he attempted to, and he consoled himself thinking that he was lucky after all, because he would die of hunger in a couple of days.

"All kinds of things come here, don Momboñombo, knives, spoons, forks, plates, everything you may need. It's a question of knowing how to search."

He continued fantasizing about dying soon. Bacán interrupted him.

"People drop things from their houses, and we put them here…"

The man observed the boy in silence, only agreeing with a nod. The boy seemed childlike to him. Everything about him made him look like a boy of seven, especially his way of speaking, and his stare, which was tender and idiotic. After a few days he noticed that Bacán would not go diving unless his mother stood watch over him. And when many people moved closer, she would take out a long rope from her bag and tie herself to the boy at the waist from the sheer terror that she might lose him. When Bacán was not diving at her side, he would spend time sitting on his stove reading anything legible he might find, or that might be given to him. He had learned to decipher words, but he was practically incapable of understanding an entire phrase. A little while after learning the mechanics of reading, the child had given himself over to the task of memorizing hundreds of words without it being possible for Única to explain their meaning to him. Now, already an adult, his immaturity was strikingly obvious to anyone outside the community, because on the inside, nobody seemed to notice it. On the contrary, more than one person was surprised by the boy's vocabulary, and the surprise that it caused made his mother swell with pride.

After dinner, the older divers retired to their shacks, and the younger ones prowled around the surrounding areas.

The dump's nights – the ones that were not abruptly interrupted by the arrival of garbage trucks during the trash high season- were dark nights, made lively only by the incessant noise of the insects and by the deep current from the sea of garbage.

From the dump's boundary toward the back, the last

vegetation on the hill survived, where all the insects took refuge to give the divers' sleep some peace of mind that something alive remained in their agonizing world.

After three weeks, Mondolfo Moya Garro had already abandoned his plan to die of hunger. He walked badly, and he had serious difficulties breathing because the divers' asthma was already affecting him.

"No one's lungs can endure this stench... and the stink of muck gets into everyone's nose and mouth without anyone realizing it..."

Única had gone over to sleep on Bacán's pieces of cardboard because she had given up her pieces to the newcomer. All three would go to bed after dinner but he did not sleep. At his side, Única and Bacán seemed to burst open from coughing. Both would speak in their sleep and they snored like a motor.

Mr. Mondolfo Moya Garro was unable to fall asleep until the early morning hours because in spite of the fact that sleep is also a disposable product, he had not managed to find even a second-hand one to brave the sleepless elements.

In the mornings, Única would rise as if she had slept in a five-star shack. At four thirty she was already on her feet, ready to go down the hill and return with her bucket filled with water. When she was able to collect a bit of money, she would wait until the neighborhood shop opened and she would buy coffee and white bread. Very rarely did her money stretch far enough to buy sugar, but that would generally come in the trucks, in the bags that people thought were empty. When she would find one, she would shout, "sssssuuugar," she would scrape out the bottom and take it out to sweeten, at the very least, Bacán's coffee.

The guest would wake up to the generous aroma of Única's cheap coffee. He would awaken breathing with difficulty and always apologizing for his frenzied return from the black hole of his sleepless nights. Waking up he had the feeling of having shouted, and that was why he would ask for forgiveness. In reality it was only a muffled sound that was not as loud as a shout, which was why Única could not understand the reason for his apology.

"Pardon for what?"

"For waking up in that ugly way."

"That is not your fault, nobody here wakes up nicely."

"Única, the coffee is a miracle."

"The miracle is that there is coffee."

Don Mondolfo's second torture, in order of importance, was his constipation. He simply could not do it, and he was already beginning to grow ill. Carmen warned him about it:

"He who does not eat, does not shit... eat more, eat more."

"It's not easy to eat with this bad odor, Oso Carmuco."

"You're new here, that's why you think everything smells. After a while you'll get used to it and nothing will ever smell like anything again."

Carmen had spoken truthfully. That odor, the product of the eternal indigestion from the land choked with trash, that putrid breath that the hill's mouth gave off, as impossible as it might seem, went unnoticed by the divers' nostrils.

"What's happening is that everything still disgusts you."

The conversations during working hours were rapid and interrupted always by the arrival of more and more trash collectors.

* * *

Don Mondolfo still wasn't diving. He would approach the edge timidly, where the waves of waste would break, and he would stand there getting his feet wet, smearing his shoes with every sticky thing that would float by him. Once in a while he would hear a shout: "Momboñoooooooombo, get in, don't be a sissy," followed by a peal of laughter.

That morning he couldn't take it any longer. He felt that his digestion had been put on automatic pilot, and he had no other choice than to run to look for a corner in some discreet part of the dump, to get relief from the very small amount he had been able to eat.

His haste dispossessed him of any modesty and propriety, and seeing that there simply did not exist any privacy in that trash dump, he was resigned to do in public what he would never have imagined. With his pants down around his ankles, and leaning against a pile of old tires, the man felt a relief like never before in his life, interrupted from time to time by the divers who were passing by there and who greeted him with the life-saving gesture- fist closed and thumb up- as if a committee of support had convened in favor of his cause. He decided not to make a big deal out of it and finished his labor in peace, responding with the same gesture to their greetings. Afterwards, a random diver approached and pointed out to him an out-of-the-way place, where some trees were standing. He thanked the diver for his discretion and for the information, but the diver, a few paces later, turned around and reminded him with a shout that that area was not a shithouse.

Once his intestines had been loosened up, he felt that he had also discarded what remained of his former condition as a citizen without any rights and with many responsibilities. Returning to Única's shack, he sat down as usual in the opening of the door and he allowed an account of his life to flood over him: a son of laborers, like almost everyone in that country that up until then he had felt as his own, orphaned at a young age, a construction worker while his strength did not fail him, a construction site guard when his strength abandoned him. Finally, a guard at the National Library, in his first "stroke of luck" that he could remember.

The last twenty-six years of his life he had lived sleeping by day and guarding by night.

Since he had gone to elementary school up to the sixth grade, he spent a couple of hours reading every night, which is why he became very familiar, for a person of his condition, with the order of the reading stacks. He loved to read old newspapers and magazines and that was how he thought the rest of his life would be.

"From the library to the cemetery," he had sworn. Once in the dump, he learned not to swear.

"What's happening here? Where are you going with those boxes of books?"

"Grandpa, don't get mixed up in this! Mind your own business. Everything has been arranged, and understand that I'm warning you."

It could only occur to don Mondolfo Moya Garro to denounce the business that the National Library administrators had with those from the company, Despish Paper, Inc., the largest toilet paper factory in the country, thanks to which tons of books and historical registers were reduced to "paper to write on with your ass," as don Mondolfo said when he uncorked the whole affair. The following day he rose to the statistics of the unemployed.

"Just like that, without any work compensation, without a right to a pension, not a damn thing. And when you're poor, not even an attorney will help, and don't even think about the union, because there isn't one for non-contractual employees."

"They gave me a filthy small unemployment benefit

so that I would stop messing with them."

"Everything went to the second-hand shops."

"You can eat less, and even not eat, but what you cannot do is not pay the house payment, because they'll put you out on the street."

"At sixty-six years of age, which is not so old, and without work, or anyone who will employ you for anything, what's left? Throw yourself into the trash!"

* * *

In the dump there ruled another order of time imposed by the flow of garbage trucks that would arrive as often as six o'clock in the morning as midnight, or in the early hours of the morning, according to the city streets' offerings of trash.

Removing himself totally from his former schedule was something that don Mondolfo never managed to do completely. Nevertheless, and miraculously, —he thought the following day— one night of so many nights he was finally able to reverse his guarding schedule and sleep continuously until around six o'clock in the morning. That morning, after witnessing the miracle of the multiplication of coffee, he finally made up his mind to become a member of the diver community's lively forces.

"How do you do it?"

"You search and throw into this bag what can be eaten, and in this other bag what can be sold."

The only two points of the instruction manual were clear, and Mondolfo Moya Garro, by midday, had already earned his next day's coffee. That noon he offered his services to go down the hill to search for water for lunch, but almost a month's growth of beard, his sticky and blackened skin from his contact with the trash, his hair impenetrable from the dust, including poverty's other attributes, were sufficient to turn his search for water into a martyrdom. From people's eyes it was easy to guess the appearance he made and the repulsion that it generated. He would not have achieved his objective if he had not taken water without permission from a gasoline station.

"Única, people look at you with disgust and with distrust… It's horrible!"

"That's because you haven't brushed your teeth since you arrived."

"But I didn't bring my brush with me!"

"Don't lie! That's not the reason. There's the toothbrush for guests and you know that you can use it."

After lunch, the man brushed his teeth and although it might be the result of pure suggestion, he felt a bit more respectable.

Brushing his teeth with the brush that Única had hanging from a shoe string on the side wall of the shack was an important step for don Mondolfo in his slow ritual of initiation into the life of the divers. Maybe not by the very act of brushing them, because apart from Única and Bacán, no other diver was doing it, but because that was how he took a qualitative jump toward overcoming his disgust, that exquisite product of high culture.

"You have to let go of that bullshit. Disgust is a luxury! As soon as hunger closes in, disgust goes away…"

"One small step for man…. an enormous step backward for mankind," he would have said if in that moment an attack of lucidity had overtaken him.

The man was abruptly torn away from his meditations by a commotion. Even within a dump the law of the strongest ruled and some groups claimed the right to sift through the recently arrived trash before the others. Única arrived with Bacán tied to her waist; she untied him and explained to the newcomer about the territorial squabbles.

"As if in hell we weren't all going to fit…"

"Momboñombo, don't say silly things, hell is here," Única answered him in one of her rare fits of socialistic realism.

"And from here I will go straight up into heaven, even though you may not believe me," she concluded in another of her frequent mystical flare-ups.

After these outbursts, she would repent for having "offended God," and she would end up making the sign of the cross and giving thanks to the Creator for her shelter and bread.

"The thing about fighting over new bags of trash, they're the result of our trade, and as you have already seen, nobody bothers me, because I am always on the alert for what each one might like. And if I find it, I go and give it to him or her, even though it may be something of value. Let's see if people will start to understand that it's not worth fighting over some worthless stuff, and that it's better to share…"

Única preached with absolute conviction her policies of pacific coexistence. But she did not overlook that her maternal figure helped her quite a bit to survive the afflictions in the dump, where all were objects without a place in the world.

To the guest the dynamics of the dump were incomprehensible. At times it seemed like a world of insanity to him, and that was when he felt the most desperate and lamented in secret that they had saved his life. At other times he felt that at least in that exile of the human condition, the constant struggle for the least thing resulted in a very different assessment of life. Of course, he did not think about it in those terms; he limited himself to murmuring something like, "the more screwed up people are, the more they hold on to life." To which Única responded, puzzled by the comment, that if everyone there sat down to feel sorry for themselves, then yes, the whole thing would seem screwed up. But dialogues between them did not last too long either.

Mr. Mondolfo had already noticed that the divers were good at going about talking to themselves and that it was difficult for them to hold a conversation for longer than five minutes. Even Única would talk to herself, and sing old school songs once in a while. She would speak to the things she would find in the trash; speaking to a tube of toothpaste, she would congratulate it for coming almost full; she would speak to a fork and introduce it to a spoon found moments before; she would rub them against her apron and put them away ceremoniously into the bag that contained the valuable things.

For his part, Bacán would spend the entire day talking to himself, repeating separate words that he would decipher from old newspapers or from the books that had run the same luck as the trash.

"Momboñombo, you have been talking to yourself for hours. What's wrong?"

* * *

"What we're missing here is air, Única. We live suffocating."

"You exaggerate so!"

That day, Mondolfo Moya Garro decided not to go out to dive. He stayed home trying to open a type of ventilation in the shack's roof. Until that moment he had not noticed the television antenna that was on the roof and it seemed to him that it couldn't be more useless. He attempted to pull it from its spot, but Bacán vigorously protested because Única had placed it on the roof as an adornment and they both enjoyed looking at it there, where it was, of course. The new air vent brought a little relief, but almost nothing to the man's sleep. Única and

Bacán did not notice the difference.

Before sleep had rescued him for a few hours from what luck had brought him, don Mondolfo thought again about the television antenna and he felt a kind of sadness mixed with tenderness that not even in a garbage dump did one lose hope of living how one supposed people ought to live, "more or less in the same way."

"If I had truly wanted to die, I would have taken poison…" It was the last thing he thought about before falling quickly into unconsciousness from fatigue.

On the toothbrush wall, Única had also hung a mirror. In the mornings don Mondolfo would wake up looking into the hell of its reflection and every day he found it more difficult to recognize himself. He would stand there looking at himself, dying to take a bath and to get off all that filth.

"The whites of my eyes are turning yellow!"

His beard was growing faster, just like his fingernails and his toenails.

"Soon my shoes won't fit and I'm not going to find any others here."

His clothes were rotting on him.

"What I wouldn't give to drink a cold beer!"

His knees hurt, his back hurt. He felt a new pain each day.

"You go to shit here right away."

He remembered the good life, and the good life for him meant his entire life of poverty, because once in the dump, even poverty seemed like a luxury.

"This isn't even poverty… it's worse."

He remembered that he used to have a canary that kept him company and that sang by day while he was sleeping before he would work at night. He hadn't thought about him since then. He remembered that on that last day, "my last day as a poor man, I had served the canary his last bit of birdseed and I left the cage open for him after thanking him and saying goodbye."

The man in the mirror was shedding tears from his eyes, he warned. The man on the other side, outside the mirror, was weeping tears that he could not let out.

"If you start to cry, it's game over!"

* * *

November was entering its third week without anyone in the dump having noticed, with the exception, of course, of don Mondolfo, who never stopped looking at the dates on the newspapers that invariably arrived one day behind. Already by the second week of his inclusion into the divers' ranks, the man was capable of guessing in which bags he could find the different periodicals.

His eyes had needed almost two months to begin to distinguish the details, to take in that at lunch time, Única would set aside a portion of food and once the table was picked up, she would take it to the elderly man who lived in the shack that was farthest away in the neighborhood.

"Who lives there, Única?"

"Don Retana, the oldest diver in the neighborhood, so old that he can no longer work."

That day the elderly man had company for lunch.

"Who is that woman who walks around with that doll tied to her back?"

"Llorona."

Llorona had arrived at the dump seven years before, with a baby a few months old in her arms.

It was an unusual story, as if fate had invented it on purpose with its lone mission to twist together once again myth and daily life in spite of the people's pain.

Llorona had arrived, like everyone there, to play her last hand of luck, and she had installed herself with the child in an improvised shack while her own was being raised. She had begun to dive almost immediately. And to reach a promising bag that was floating far from the shore, she left the child in a clearing amid the garbage not having the least idea that there was nothing less trustworthy in the dump than those ephemeral spaces. On her return, after two or three minutes, she could not find him. Two or three hours later, the woman went completely mad. Even the tractors stopped their progress, because it was as if the universe had come to a complete stop. The police came to answer the call the administration had made. Everyone suspended his or her labors. At nightfall the child was given up for lost. The woman never recuperated from her tragedy. She stayed to live in the shantytown and she spent all her time turning over the trash, always crying. Often she rolled the trash around at night and her sobbing frightened the resident divers. When Llorona's sobs penetrated Única's deep sleep, she would get up, she would look for her in the darkness, she would calm her down, and finally she would convince her to return home. Única would not return until she left her sleeping and tucked in.

"At other times it's Oso Carmuco who gets up and goes looking for her, takes her home and there they have relations."

Don Mondolfo could scarcely give credence to the story he had just heard. But just as he observed new situations, he would also listen to stories that he would have preferred never to hear.

"Única, have you seen a sweet couple over there in the trash, a slim young girl who always goes around with a skinny young man…?"

"Those are the Novios, that's what we call them."

Somebody gave them the name of "newlyweds," because they got married so young, so young that no matter how many years they accumulated, they never stopped looking like those young newlywed couples who kiss each other on the buses. They were so young, so young that no matter how many years of service they accumulated, neither did they stop looking like those employees who never get a promotion. Their little house was so small, so small, that it never stopped looking like those houses where children play at being adults.

Novio was let go first, so they continued to live on Novia's salary. And they decided definitively to give up coffee because not only did they consider it to be a superfluous expenditure, it was their only superfluous expenditure.

It took a month and three weeks to overcome the torment of their brains asking them for at least one cup a day.

By the fourth week from that second month, Novia was let go. By the fifth week from that second month, their electricity was cut off. By the seventh week from that second month, their water was shut off. By the ninth week from that second month, they were evicted.

A neighbor gave them a medium sized bag of coffee, so they also took their coffee maker and, as if knowing it beforehand, without saying anything to each other, the Novios took each other's hands and set off for the shantytown.

They were lucky. One of the shacks was abandoned.

Novio began to unwrap the bundle. Novia stretched out the blankets and shook them. Novio went back to the little house and he returned with more things wrapped in the last blanket. Novia had procured several cardboard boxes, so they laid down the bed. Novio improvised a stove with the rusty ring from a bus wheel that he found around there. Novia observed that they did not have anything to cook. Novio went for water, lit the fire, and poured out a nice bit of coffee. They drank it without sugar and they settled in to sleep.

They had never been in a shantytown.

They could not sleep, even though each one pretended so as not to awaken the other.

Toward early morning, the Novios were still awake and they were trembling. He turned to her side, embraced her and told her: "It's because of the coffee… we had gotten used to not drinking it!"

Don Mondolfo found out about their story first hand. Novio recounted it to him in detail when he asked him how they had turned up there. Likewise, he told him his own story and they became friends.

"Ah, and you thought they were here out of sheer pleasure!"

One day, a doll the size of a baby arrived inside a trash bag. A baby carrier came with the doll. Única and Bacán were in the process of evaluating the find when Llorona fell on top of them, shrieking with her eyes bulging. She snatched the toy away from them and left, shutting herself up with it in her shack. Nobody dared to enter until three days later when she was too weak to put up any more resistance. They found her sitting on the ground, dehydrated, singing an almost imperceptible lullaby and breast-feeding the doll.

Única took care of her for a few days, showed her how to put the doll into the carrier and how to carry it on her back.

"But she still cries and looks for the child in the garbage…!"

"Well, of course! She may be crazy, but she's not stupid."

* * *

The few pick-up trucks that remained would collect the less desirable trash from the city's poor neighborhoods. In one of them an old rusty cot arrived one morning. Don Mondolfo saw it and he felt a knot in his throat. He armed himself with a shovel, he brandished it in the air and shouted: "The cot is mine!" Not even the young divers dared to fight over the coveted prize with the newcomer because he was so determined to get back at least the dignity of sleeping in a bed.

Don Mondolfo, Carmen and Novio arrived at Única's home with the pieces from the cot and between the three of them they put it together. The cot was too large for the shack, which was why they dedicated the following days to remodeling the bedroom. They had to tear down the back wall and put it up again a few feet away to make room for the queen-sized cot, which in that moment became the principle piece of furniture in the house. Of course, don Mondolfo forgot one small detail: it was neither fair that he should sleep in such a big and comfortable bed while Única and Bacán shared their pieces of cardboard, nor would it be proper for Única to sleep in the same bed with a man. Who would have cared? Nobody, of course; but it mattered to Única because she had not renounced her respectability, no matter how often cruel reality had shown her for more than twenty years that values cannot be eaten.

"This is a decent house!"

Don Mondolfo Moya Garro continued to sleep on the ground.

Única almost melted when he relinquished his cot to her and helped her to lay down the cardboard so that she and Bacán could sleep there.

That night both mother and son slept like kings, and they coughed less. Don Mondolfo wiped away two large tears that rolled down his cheeks; perhaps from the touching scene, perhaps from seeing himself again lying down on his pieces of cardboard on the opposite side of the shack.

"At least at night the tractors don't always make noise."

The infernal racket of those machines, persistent, uninterrupted, pounding; it still felt like agony to him that he had to suffer in silence, because each time he mentioned it he would always receive the answer, "What noise?" What noise? What smell? What flies? The divers did not spend their lives swishing away flies, nor closing their noses so as not to breathe in the foul-smelling trash. He had noticed that even Única would put on perfume each morning, and the noise did not keep her from singing softly to herself all day long. She stirred into a large bottle the mortal remains of any perfume she might find, without caring if the fragrances were for men or for women, or if the scents were incompatible with each other. She would stir them together with an alchemist's artistry and she would concoct unprecedented aromas, which luckily were unnoticeable to those who were close by once she dived into the depths of the dump. The community's divers would voluntarily turn over to her any florid scent that might appear there. All that belonged exclusively to Única Oconitrillo.

"End of the month, Mr. Momboñombo Moña Gallo!"

That meant it was harvest time. They had to go down to the city to sell bottles and cans to the recyclers and, with the earnings, go shopping for our daily coffee and cookies from the bakery and...

Mondolfo Moya Garro's face fell. Until that moment the idea of returning to the world ever again in this lifetime had not even crossed his mind. Walking again along the streets he had known his whole life...now with his wretched appearance, his clothes in rags, his hair matted and his beard overgrown.

"Única, I'm not going. I am staying here to take care of the house."

"Don't talk nonsense, Momboñombo. Where there is nothing, everything is safe."

Única headed the procession, followed by Bacán, each one with his or her sack. Don Mondolfo came along a few steps behind carrying a sack of beer cans and another sack of bottles, and even further back were Carmen, Novio and Novia, all prepared to earn their bread with the sweat of their brow.

The street was not the same. The people were not the same, nor the cars, nor the usual buildings, nor Central Park. The city was not the same seen from the perspective of a diver, which don Mondolfo had become. His preoccupation that someone might recognize him was painfully dispelled when he ran smack into an old acquaintance who did not answer the timid greeting he had given him. Quite simply, Mr. Moya Garro had disappeared from the world of the living and it had not occurred to anyone to inform the police, or to give him up for lost…not even his old acquaintances or his distant relatives; nobody noticed his departure into the exile of the dregs of society.

His companions, in turn, were saying hello and were greeted by the people on the streets, by the so-called "informal economy," the street vendors, and by the lottery ticket sellers, the beggars, the bus drivers, and the Central Park preachers. On almost every corner there was someone greeting Única, Carmen, Bacán and all of them together because they were recognized as a group. Like Mondolfo, no one was there to greet The Newlyweds either.

"Única, who is that man who said hello to you…that one, the one in a monk's habit, the one who was carrying a sign in his hand?"

"That man is Father Jerónimo the Worst, a wise man."

"I always thought he was a crazy man! I've seen him for years on the streets…"

In that moment, don Mondolfo Moya Garro saw his entire body in the mirror of a clothing store's display window. He stopped paralyzed. His pitiful appearance hadn't left anything of his former self.

"I look like a crazy man!"

"Momboñoooooombo, don't just stand there, get moving."

"Don't shout at me Oso Carmuco!"

The man could not stop thinking that if instead of throwing himself into the trash, if he had thrown himself from the roof of the General Library, for example; it wouldn't have made any difference. What he could not believe was that not even his very few friends had missed him, nor had reported his disappearance. He mentioned his sorrow to Única.

"When you end up in the trash, nobody looks for you… So, stop thinking about all that."

"We're nothing!"

Carmen heard the old man's complaint, and he began to repeat the famous statement imitating his voice and walking like a drunk.

The hike through the city's downtown was torture for don Mondolfo. He had to submit to his companions' group dynamics, which apart from that were incomprehensible. The divers were walking awkwardly, as if the pavement's solid ground destabilized them; as if they missed the garbage dump's shifting terrain. They would stop to rummage through the trash cans on the sidewalks and sometimes the store clerks would come out to run them off, because they would leave trash strewn about that was of no use to them. They would cross the street challenging the cars that were bearing down on them. The only thing that worried Única was Bacán's safety, which was why she was leading him attached to her waist with that umbilical nylon cord, accentuating even more his appearance as "a young man with problems."

The return to the garbage dump, toward the end of the afternoon, was for don Mondolfo what he would never have imagined: the feeling of returning home. He took off his shoes, he loosened his shirt and his belt and he fell exhausted onto his cardboard. He did not even get up for dinner.

The following day there was coffee for breakfast; there were cookies from the bakery and a rare luxury! Scrambled eggs.

"It's almost December, Momboñombo!"

"And how do you know, if you never even know the date?"

Única sighed deeply...

"Well, I don't know. I just feel something like

uneasiness when Christmas approaches!"

The shantytown had grown noticeably in those twenty years. For its twenty-first anniversary, its population had already multiplied to capacity; but since misery knows no limits, more and more people were arriving to the summit of waste to try their luck...to test their bad luck.

Poverty had reached the top of the hill and from there it was already threatening to spill down over the rest of the citizenry, the day in which not even one more bag would fit in the dump nor the diver that would search through it.

Many divers would arrive and they would leave without deciding on whether to make their home in the shantytown. They were people who were diving in the streets of the city; unmistakable due to their attire, their delicate gait, their scrutinizing stare, their obstetrician's touch, specialized by virtue of recognizing the interior of a trash bag by carefully validating the contents of its belly without breaking it, and with a class awareness that trained them to distinguish at a glance the rich neighborhood's trash from that of the poor neighborhoods.

* * *

"The rain showers won't let up!" said Única when the end of November seemed more like the beginning of October.

"What's bad is that even the rain comes down on the dump already used and dirty," added Mondolfo Moya Garro.

It had begun to rain in April that year, and they had already endured several tropical waves and cold fronts that for the poor always meant triple the cold, and they undermined the health of those people on board. Bacán was coughing constantly and his nose was always running, turning his mustache green and making his beard stiff.

The rain trickled down the buzzards' oily black top feathers and everywhere pools formed creating thousands of small lagoons between the plastic bags. When November's paltry sun hit them, the little lagoons, fecund with fly larvae and other critters, would shine with prisms of light and they stank. The colorful display gave the impression that they had murdered the rainbow and that its dead body was slowly rotting in the trash.

With so much rain, the divers became drenched no matter how much they covered themselves with improvised rain coats made from plastic bags. The shacks would flood and so they had to alternate the diving work with the floating city's interminable repairs up and down the dump.

Dressed in gray, with garden-sized plastic bags turned into rain jackets, and a cord tied around their waists, the divers looked like a sect worshiping the end of the world. Their plastic habits on their backs, always hunched over, completed a hazy image of a penitents' pilgrimage under the supervision of the tractors.

"In summer everything will be easier," Mr. Moya Garro would repeat while standing drinking directly from the clouds' utters. He was still not acquainted with the sun's effects in February and March on the dump's rotting and loamy soil, which in that moment was a torrent of mud draining blood minute by minute from the parts of the hill still alive. The green areas were drifting away day by day, as if even the trees were leaving on their own accord from that vault of bones of the human condition.

Bacán would entertain himself floating little paper boats in the small lagoons nearest the shack. The rest of the children divers scavenged in the trash with as much ferocity as the adults, but with a different expression, with astonishment in their eyes as if what they were looking for without knowing it was nothing less than their own childhood left to rot in the waste.

The persistent rain loosened the landfill's soil. After standing a moment in the same place, the divers had to pull up hard because their legs would be already up to their knees in mud. Twenty years, more or less, of burying trash at that site, had turned the hill into a nightmarish monstrosity; mounds everywhere and earth dug up from one side to another, and the rivers Damas and Tiribí were condemned to drink the broth from the constant filtration that was intravenously injected into the earth's body.

* * *

"Sol-i-lar-itty… sol-ilarity… solidarity."

"What are you reading, Bacán?"

"The newspaper."

"May I see it?"

RÍO AZUL'S RESIDENTS ASK GOVERNMENT FOR SOLIDARITY

"Sol-ilarity, sol-ilarity… I can't say that word, Momboñombo!"

"Well, it's a very complicated word… Look, Bacán, only they know the government is going to help them…"

"Sol-i-larity… sol-ilarity… solidarity."

"Momboñombo, are you talking to yourself again?"

"No. I am speaking with Bacán."

"Oh!"

"Sol-ilarity, sol-ilarity, sol…"

"Shut up, Bacán!"

"Don't wear yourself out. Now he's going to spend hours upon hours repeating that stupid word."

* * *

At the beginning, at the very beginning, she had planted a garden. She had planted it little by little with plants that the people from Río Azul gave her, when they still did not distrust the divers too much, when they did not even call them "divers," but rather "the people who live in tiny huts, over there in the dump."

She planted morning glories so they would climb and wind around the back of the shack. And in what was called "the patio," she had planted oregano, long coriander and lemon grass. In what was called "the garden," which was nothing more than the front of the shack, she had planted begonias and gloxinias in powdered milk tins. That was where she stubbornly and uselessly attempted to plant her white rose bush. She tied some purple orchids to a hallow heart stick, since it was a custom in her family. She adopted a turtle that had come there one day, and she filled the walkway along the road with white impatiens to make believe that they were white roses from the rose bush.

It was during those garden years when Bacán appeared.

She had always wanted to have a son, and that was why she took charge of the child as the most conclusive proof of God's goodness who, informed of her wish, had made the child especially for her and was going to leave him for her a few steps from her home.

Deprived by nature of the dignity of roses, which categorically refused to live in the dump, the impatiens grew, multiplied and blossomed before the last cutting was reduced to a dry stick that had to be removed from the road so that Bacán would not prick his fingers.

In front of the white flowers, Única taught Bacán to recite:

"*I grow a white rose, in June as in January, for the sincere friend who gives me his honest hand. And for the cruel friend who tears out my beating heart, I grow neither thistle nor nettle: I grow a white rose.*"

"Beautiful! Isn't it, Momboñombo? I don't know who wrote it, but it must be someone who really liked to make gardens. I taught it to Bacán because I have never lost faith in having a rose bush. That's why I always recite that passage, and surely you have heard Bacán reciting it too, because when you recite it, it's as if we had the garden here. I know that the man who wrote it surely must have made gardens where they only threw away trash, because to write such a passage, so pretty, you really have to love roses and your friends…"

But the land was drying up. It was dying. The dump was extending irrevocably as the tractors were digging deeper and deeper to deal with the space. Soon even the trees abandoned the place and the land turned to clay and the air turned sticky.

The turtle suffocated in the dust, with the plants and the flowers, and the white impatiens sank along the road with everything else. And the world, their world, turned yellowish and treacherous. The cockroaches multiplied infinitely and the flies formed an opaque film that allowed the sun's light to shine through only with difficulty.

"Afterwards life goes on and you start to grow old, isn't that right, Momboñombo? Bacán, each day bigger, it's true! I tell him to shave that beard, but he doesn't like to because he cuts himself, and because the blades come here rusty and without an edge. Although now it's easier, because they come attached to the shaving razors... Poor little Llorona...! If I had lost Bacán, I would have gone crazy too... Oh, Momboñombo! You keep looking at me and you pay so much attention to me it makes me feel like talking and talking the whole night... and it has been so long since I had anyone to talk to, overall like this, at night, after everyone has left for their homes..."

Don Mondolfo Moya Garro remained silent for quite a while. He was listening to that woman who seemed transported, with her eyes fixed on the wall, speaking about the garden years like someone who talks about the good old days, which he considered to be admirable.

"Before we used to go diving over there, in the city. But it's very tiring because you have to walk the entire day and people give you dirty looks when they see you open their trash bags. As if they didn't see that it's trash, as if they still needed the things after they had thrown them away! They don't say anything to the men, but when they see a woman, then, they run her around everywhere, even if she has a small child to feed. Momboñombo, you know that I have come to the conclusion that trash is also a woman... Look, it's trash- in feminine gender. I know about gender because I used to teach it in school. So, it's trash, and in the beginning, it was pleasing to all, when it was nice and new, and as soon as it grows old, then, no one wants it…But that's how people are and that's why I prefer to dive here alone. Then you go over there and sell what you find…"

* * *

"RÍO AZUL'S RESIDENTS ANNOUNCE ULTIMATUM TO GOVERNMENT"

"Ul-tiii-maaa-tum, ultiii-maaa-tum, ulti-matum…"

"Bacán, be quiet!"

"Oso Carmuco says that story is older than the habit of shitting while sitting down…"

"Don't talk so filthy in front of the boy!"

"The thing is that the residents of Río Azul and San Antonio de Desamparados have never wanted this trash dump in their neighborhood, Única. You know that they're right!"

"Of course, since they're not the ones living here…!"

December had already taken possession of the calendar. It was felt by the somewhat colder wind and by the decrease in the sticky rains from the previous months. Now only a slight drizzle was falling that scarcely trickled down the divers' skin.

Christmas always arrived at the dump without any cover-up, like the colorful vomit of commercialism that it is; and in its own way, that goddamn season was generous to the community of divers.

It is the season when people are more careless than usual about what they throw out. An unimaginable variety of things would always come tangled up in the tamale leaves; all kinds of silverware, expensive and cheap, and even a set of dentures that a diver hung around his neck like a trophy of war. Wrapping papers, enough to wrap up the entire garbage dump and return it to its rightful owners, did not always come empty; often they were intact, with the gift inside, as if someone had thought about the amazement of the diver who might find it, so much more profound if it were a child. And the thing, lost forever, it would be resurrected, filled with life in his hands, and for a second it would conjure up for him the illusion that not everything in life was the same old shit. But rarely did such a valuable prize fall into children's hands. Generally, the adult divers' trained eyes rapidly recognized that kind of merchandise, and the fate of the lost gift would be some thrift shop in the city.

People feel strange in December, all the people, even the "un-people," the ones who live from waste, from remains, from carelessness, damage, mistakes, and wastefulness ... those unfortunate ones to whom don Mondolfo Moya Garro, under his enormously long pseudonym, had joined his efforts to pretend that life, after all, was worthwhile even when it was lived in the middle of unpredictability. A somewhat conservative position that more than one diver would often argue with him and for which he earned insults from time to time:

"Look at it, life is worthwhile? Momboñombo, don't be stupid. Life is a punishment."

And the old man would pull on his hair searching for arguments, but everything that came to his mind would have been more useful to demonstrate scientifically that poverty was the worst load of crap ever invented, than to convince his listener that the idea about punishment would offend God.

Mondolfo Moya Garro no longer remembered how long it had been since he joined the ranks of the bio-recyclers, in part because time was something that more and more mattered less to him. In fact, he had even given his wristwatch to Bacán (the only thing from his belongings that did not end up in the second-hand shop), and neither did he bother to teach him how to read it nor did the other ask him about the fascinating game of the watch hands turning and turning without any purpose.

That year, Christmas came early to the dump. During the first days of December, Río Azul was declared a "Protected Zone," and the one hundred and fifty-eight acres that the dump covered were annexed to the Cerro de la Carpintera zone, which elevated the status of the place like never before, even being declared under the Department of Forestry. The divers would never have found out anything if it hadn't been for Mr. Moya Garro who caught the news in a newspaper that was on its way to the campfire, not due to the death sentence that it surely deserved, but because it was time to cook dinner.

"What is the Department of Forestry?"

A question the old man saw coming:

"Here it says that this zone is going to be protected now."

"From what?"

"Well… no one can cut down trees any longer without permission…"

"But there aren't any trees here!"

"Well… then no one can come here any longer to kill animals…"

Única thought seriously about it. She remained silent a good while and finally came to a conclusion.

"How great that no one will come here any longer to kill buzzards, or rats, or cockroaches, because they are also God's creatures!"

Since irony was not common in her, Mondolfo nodded respectfully, although not very convinced due to the bit of laughter that escaped from her while she was delivering the newspaper to its well-earned torment from the flames.

The newspapers carried the news for a month, talking about the local residents' discontent and about the street blockades they were making in protest of the more than twenty years of government neglect regarding the dump site. One of the blockades of the access road to the dump had already caused an accumulation of trash in the streets of San José.

MOUNTAINS OF TRASH
RESIDENTS OF RÍO AZUL THREATEN
TO CARRY ON BLOCKADE"

Colorful photographs… people jumping over the mounds of trash in the heart of the capital, people holding their noses with their hands, fed up with so much filth.

Mondolfo showed the photograph to Única. She understood why the influx of garbage collectors had dropped off in the dump.

"Thank goodness! I was so scared."

For Mondolfo, Única's fear was evident as never before; previously he had been in the ranks of those who hold their noses when it smells like trash.

"Of course, trash only exists for people when it begins to get in their way!"

* * *

The residents of Río Azul and of San Antonio de Desamparados had threatened the government with blocking the access road to the dumpsite around the thirty-first of December. It was a conflict almost as old as the dump, but never as acute as then, because the trash had already exceeded the site's capacity. With more than enough reasons, the residents were demanding its immediate closure.

"Jesus, Mary and Joseph, and where are they going to put it?"

"That's the million dollar question. There is nowhere to construct a new dump. People are not as dumb as the Government thinks. Nobody wants to have a garbage dump of that size around one's house. They wanted to build it in La Uruca. The people threatened. They said that México Hospital was there, the National Amusement Park... how should I know, Única. Everything is around there, so the Government doesn't know where to put this shithole. Única, the residents are right."

"Fine, yes, but don't say it so ugly like that because this is where we live."

Not content with the declaration of a "Protected Zone," the residents of Río Azul maintained their ultimatum.

The Government, for its part, was not doing anything other than stuffing Santa Clause's bag even more, with nothing less than the proposal to relocate the dump to another city's neighborhood or to some other part of the country.

"What does yesterday's newspaper say today, Momboñombo?"

"It says that the trash is a problem of negative externalities."

"My God! And what is that?"

"The Devil must know what it is."

"What are we going to do, Momboñombo? What are we going to live on?"

The question was taking on dimensions ever more gigantic in Mondolfo's head. He was going about talking about the problem to the divers, without provoking in them more than laughter from his frightened face. He wasn't a diver; he was a frustrated suicide who refused to admit for even a moment the possibility that his new life's meaning might be snatched from his hands. He still did not dare to confess that he even had affection for the dump, and for its people.

The divers for their part, the real divers, those who had arrived at the dump many years ago with a hollow soul, and who by now had already stuffed it with trash, the authentic divers did not understand Mondolfo's concerns. They were used to living day to day. They were not even like Única, who after so many years had still not been able to relinquish her traditions and she continued to attempt family frameworks within the community. The problem did not worry them, they did not understand it, nor did they want to understand it; furthermore, the topic was already starting to bore them, so they didn't do anything more than laugh at the old man. Nevertheless, they did not stop going to Única's house toward the close of evening with some kind of contribution for the common pot. They would sit down to have dinner in a group as if led by some archaic family order that worked for them like the habit works for the pet dog when scraping the ground with his hind legs after taking a crap, as if he were burying his shit with that useless gesture.

The divers simply did not understand that man's anxiety.

"It's people spreading rumors…"

"They will never close this place, grandpa, don't you see that if they close it they won't have anywhere to throw out this trash…"

"Okay, but if they close it, what then?"

"If they close it, nothing. We'll go wherever they put it."

"And if they don't let us in?"

"Grandpa, don't be silly. Yes, they're going to let us in, yes they're going to let us. They always say the same thing, that they´re not going to let us come in, and I don´t know what else; but in the end they always let us. And you sir, stop screwing up your life with that stuff."

And that was how all of Mondolfo's attempts died trying to create a consciousness in the divers. In short, what he was demanding from them was that if they had saved him from death, then they should not let him die now that he was getting enjoyment from it all again.

* * *

Río Azul's residents were blocking the streets trying to impede the trash collectors' access. On their end, the police were sending in riot squads to open up the passage again.

The local residents were burning tires and the police were throwing tear gas and other arguments of that nature, until the community finally succeeded in getting the Government to accept a dialogue.

Mr. President of the Republic in person, don Junior María Caldegueres, met with the community leaders; he brought them pastries to go with their coffee, and he convinced them to continue their negotiations with the President's Chief of Staff.

Mondolfo got up earlier that day. He did a good job of brushing his teeth. He brushed off his old jacket as far as it was possible for him, and he sat down to wait for the time of the meeting to attend as a representative of the community of divers.

"Única, of course they're going to let me go in, since I even met old Caldegueres during the time of the revolution. When I tell Junior María that I was his dad's friend, of course he is going to let me go in."

"You were a friend of Junior María, the old man! I don't even believe you about that, and look, I believe almost everything from you."

The Chief of Staff asked for a postponement of several months in order to resolve the location problem of the new landfill. The local residents were insisting on the dump's closure by the thirty-first of December.

"Some enormous men with dark glasses did not let me approach the President, Única, but if he had seen me..."

* * *

The community of Atenas was on permanent alert because that name was being tossed around as a possible new location for all the trash from the Greater Metropolitan Area. The inhabitants of Atenas were threatening a new Trojan War if they attempted to put the landfill in their town, and the Government was promising that it would be a model landfill, like never before seen in Latin America, a garbage dump with the latest technology, like those in the United States, where even the rats eat with a knife and fork.

"They're closing it, closing it..." Mondolfo Moya Garro went about repeating to any diver who would give him one minute of his attention; but not more than a minute, which was the longest amount of time the divers managed to fix their attention on something that was not of their immediate interest.

While the phantom of the dump's closing was growing in his chest, the old man would dive shoulder to shoulder with Única and at times also with Bacán. "Única is looking worn out," he would think when he got distracted looking at her for a long time... The last rains of the year, those that catch everyone off guard, came down in large drops along her tangled threads of graying hair, and slid down the skin of her arms to her gloves without fingers that she once found around there, which she added forever to her diving gear.

"Ah, Momboñombo, stop watching me, there's nothing in my face that's worthwhile."

She said it blushing just a bit, with a sweet little smile that turned into the respite he had been yearning for so intensely. It was as if in that second the noise of the tractors stopped and the fetid fluids dissipated. It was as if the rain had stopped falling. Her complicit smile injected him with a dose of good humor. But the pause did not last more than a second. Immediately the old man and woman returned to their work.

"Just like that, pulling and pulling in the same direction, like two good little oxen," as Única was showing how the work was done.

Generally, that instant of enchantment was shattered when a new garbage truck went through the looking glass and made its triumphant entrance into un-wonderland and the divers multiplied around it like seagulls over a fishing boat. The nets arrived full and the brawny sailors from the city's asphalt sea emptied them in the middle of screeches and beating wings from those seagulls fallen on hard times. One of them took a prize in its beak and fled at full speed, but another larger seagull soon caught it. They rolled over each other on the ground and in the end the winner took flight with the spoils won in the uneven battle. When the fishing boat was empty, the captain gave the order to weigh anchor, it reversed gears and moved away toward new harbors.

They found Bacán sitting in the trash bawling like crazy. An unfriendly diver had snatched something from him and he did not know how to explain clearly what it was, or why he wanted it. Única armed herself with a broomstick and she went directly to take on the thief. Her age and the respect that strangely enough they gave her in the dump, allowed her to teach the big seagull a lesson with a beating, and to return home unharmed with a badly beaten up telephone that Bacán had rescued from the trash. The boy stopped crying.

"The next time you leave it to me," Mondolfo told Única with great dignity in the privacy of their home after dark. He said it with an authentic conviction of manhood that although implausible did not stop Única from thanking him, even if it were only out of courtesy. Because a woman who had spent twenty years teaching destiny a lesson with a thrashing did not need a knight-errant to come and defend her. What Única was thanking him for was his solidarity, which for her was priceless.

"Sol-ilarity, sol-i-larity, soli-dari-ty. Sol-ilarity…"

"Damn!" Bacán had awakened.

* * *

"Única, what if we speak with the neighbors!"

"Speak about what?"

"What about what! And what would it be about, girl? The stuff about the closing of the dump… If we were allied with the neighbors!"

"If we were what?"

"If we were allied, if we made an alliance…"

"Ah, an alliance! … It's just that I haven't heard that word since I was forbidden from going back to Mass."

"If we offered them support in their fight to close the dump…"

"Now you really have gone crazy, Momboñombo! If they close the dump, what are we going to do?"

"That's what it's about, woman. If we become unemployed, the Government is going to have to decide how to deal with us. Look, we're going to their next meeting with the Secretary, and we'll tell them that we agree with them, that this damn thing has to be closed; but we can't be without a trade or benefits, we need help, we have rights, like everyone else, we're not here because we like flies and bad odors, or because we can't do anything but wallow in trash. Look, I can offer them my services as a guard in some place, and you, as a teacher, and those who don't know how to do anything, well they can be taught something there… something, and…"

Única hadn't imagined that a heart like hers, which had already been crusted over from so much suffering, could crumble so easily from just listening to that good man's ravings. The pain wrapped her in a clammy drowsiness. A few minutes later she was snoring as if dreams were possible.

The old man fell asleep a little later with the conviction of having found the solution to the problem.

Bacán had been sleeping for a while, hugging the telephone returned to him, as if this useless thing were a teddy bear and not the sad omen of the fate of the country's telecommunications.

The trash dump had fully succumbed after another uneven battle… another day of fruitless labor.

The divers were sleeping, the flies were sleeping, and the rats, and the buzzards. The tractors were sleeping, and all the trash in its lethal broth, and sleep made everyone equal, rats and people, in the same conditions.

Río Azul's residents, not without more than enough reasons, were sick and tired of the divers. In fact, one of the agreement's clauses with the Government was that once the dump was closed, squatter settlements would not be permitted in order to declare the area a "Forest Reserve" and to regain the land.

Even though by biblical decree, "the poor will always be with you," nobody there was willing to tolerate any longer the presence of the divers wandering around their houses, stealing their trash, spoiling the countryside with their apocalyptic faces and their pitiful rags. In the end, poverty can't be blamed on the people… or can it?

* * *

Mondolfo's alliance would not have occurred even to Mother Theresa. Río Azul's community was fighting fiercely to get rid of that odious mountain with all its forms of life included.

The logic was always simple and it was always the same: Why the hell, if between all of us we produce the trash, only one town has to be stuck with it? It couldn't be more obvious.

Again, Mondolfo "got up in the wee hours," as old Caldegueres used to say; he brushed his teeth well and went down the hill in search of the community leaders; and as if written in the stars, they did not pay attention to him. They only saw a ragged diver muttering something incomprehensible.

"They didn't even look at me!"

In her own way, Única had warned him about that, foreseeing the effects of rejection in the good man's spirit.

"I don't hold a grudge against them… they are right."

Defeated, disheartened, with glassy eyes, he started the trip back and along the way he would tell the story to anyone who had the bad luck to bump into him.

"Surely I would have done the same, if I had been blessed with a different fate."

The divers listened to his story for thirty seconds before remembering that the old man was half crazy, as they believed.

"Not all divers are decent people, and who is going

to deny it…"

"The divers are a plague," the community leaders were explaining to the Secretary's delegate. They say filthy things to the neighborhood girls, they steal what they see, they break open trash bags, they urinate on the walls…

It was Sunday and the old man had not realized it. All the residents of Río Azul were in their homes, the doors were open and in almost all of them a radio was blaring, at a more than excessive volume, the unpardonable broadcast of a soccer match.

A goal sung with the force of a Hallelujah reached all of Mondolfo's five senses.

The old man stopped. On his face the complicit smile appeared automatically by which fans identify each other even though they may never have seen each other. He smiled with a happiness drawn from the past. He was a new man; his spirit reached its highest level in recent months.

Soccer does not recognize differences between the members of its brotherhood… With all the rights of ownership, Mondolfo ventured a little in the direction of the door from where the sports announcer´s redemptive shout had originated. A group of men gripping their beers still had not finished celebrating when…

"How's the game going, boys…!"

They shut the door in his face.

There was something still worse than the failure of

the alliance and that was not even being worthy of being told how the damned shitty game was going, which was not going to solve any of his problems, but for an instant his soul had rejoiced, because that's what the foolish soul does.

One more *No* in his existence was only an imperceptible link in his life of negations. But not even being worthy of their telling him who was playing against whom, or even what the score was?

"Those sons of bitches."

He wasn't even allowed the tranquilizing drug of a soccer match.

"How hard would it have been for them?"

All, all the soccer matches that he had seen and listened to throughout his life became a lump in his throat. All, all the damned goals that he had suffered through or celebrated, all the hours dedicated to the prompt reading of the sports reports clogged him up in the you know where. Thousands of men kicking thousands of balls, mountains of people roaring in the stands; bags of urine, fries, a wave of shit that was like the confirmation of soccer's brotherhood, obscene posturing between the players each time they scored, street fights at the exits, violent fans, a gunshot from time to time, some dead man from time to time… crazed announcers testifying to the same thing that everyone witnessed, battalions of fiendish referees intoning the march of hell with their whistles.

Parades of automobiles through the streets celebrating that goal scored in a foreign country for the pride of all posterity, and the legacy of those not yet born, and the President of the Republic prancing through the streets on a work day declared a holiday as the result of a kick, and entire forests reduced to newspaper by the ancient feat of David and Goliath, because we had walloped one of the great ones, we, yes, we, an example to the world, one hundred years of democracy, so they don't think that we're just some pretty faces. "Take that!" shouted Junior María Caldegueres, ensuring the pardon of sins, the salvation of his soul and eternal life. But while Goliath was crying aloud that they stop the world so he could get off, from the fucking shame, they shoved up into David, without Vaseline, a packet of new taxes that he could not remove either with the slingshot or with the rock. And don Mondolfo Moya Garro in the middle of Central Park was crying from gratitude because all men had become brothers, and we were speaking in plural, and we were in the eye of the world, and it was already almost unnoticeable how third world we were, and the Scots be damned because we had made them eat dust... "Fucking damn huge goal so that it hurts them more." And the miracle of turning water into guaro and the multiplication of chicharrón snacks, and the national hangover that would come the following day after the grand finale from El Conejo and...

"And they slammed the door on me!"

It was too much, he collapsed in the middle of the street and was carried to his new home in the arms of a pair of divers who found him discarded there, as usual.

The entire terrain of Única's heart came to a full stop when she saw him coming, pale as the Resurrected Man, in the arms of two men from those on board. They massaged the back of his neck with alcohol and they loosened his clothing so that he could breathe easier. They gave Bacán a drink of salt water to help him get over his fright, and between all of them they brought the old man back, with slaps and shouts. It took him awhile to put everything in order again in his brain's little office wastebasket.

Once he had recuperated from the mishap, he related the whole thing about the failure of the alliance and about the other thing there was only a void… he forgot forever that he had always liked soccer.

* * *

For lunch there was beef stew with vegetables.

Every Sunday at the first glimmer of light, Única and Bacán would go down the hill in the direction of the Farmers Market in Desamparados.

"There are always good people, aren´t there, Bacán?"

She was carrying two large bags; he, two small ones.

"They know they can't sell everything… and since they're country people they're not likely to waste anything, much less food."

From stand to stand, from stall to stall.

"Can you spare something for me?"

"Take this, doña Única, but put that bum to work."

"Ingrate! Don't you see that he's only a boy!

From Sunday to Sunday.

"That papaya, yes, that one, the one that's too ripe! May the Lord repay you!"

From shame to shame.

At the end of the morning they took one last turn around the market picking up what had remained on the ground, vegetables thrown away from carelessness or because they were rotten, whichever it might be.

A butcher shop provided meat for the divers' table, surviving from the times of the hatchet and the pale-faced butcher. It was a business with no future or progress, not at all competitive without electric saws to cut up bones, without electric grinders to grind the meat. It was the last artisan butcher shop in San Antonio de Desamparados, and one might say the last master butcher. The man would give Única the nameless parts of the cow, the leftovers that not even forensic pathology could identify, but in the dump's common pot it went back to just being meat.

Sunday's remaining hours transpired uneventfully in the middle of the disturbing silence of a day off. The tractors rested lifelessly at the foot of the hill, and the garbage trucks in their respective communities.

Only the thousands upon thousands of the flies'

beating wings held the routine afloat; and against the sky, like damned angels sewn into the heavens, the ever-faithful buzzards.

The divers who did not live in the shantytown disappeared even from the residents' memory. The city swallowed them and left them in suspended animation, sleeping on the sidewalks, blanketed in their garden trash bags, like enormous larvae of some species waiting for extinction.

Mondolfo, still somewhat pale, noticed the silence that day, the dump's slowing wave, the distant breeze over the trees from the crusty coast. He vaguely remembered his Sundays.

"I'm dying for a cold beer."

"Well for sure there isn´t one here."

"And if I ask God for one!"

"If God went around handing out beer, nobody would return to work."

"It doesn´t matter to us if people work or not."

"That's a lie! If people did not work, they would have nothing to throw out, and we nothing to eat."

* * *

That year Bacán's birthday was celebrated in the middle of December.

"But, why? Doesn't he celebrate his birthday in the same month like everyone else?"

"Well, no! And he is not like everyone else."

The random celebration was due to the impossibility of knowing the month and the day Bacán had come into the world.

"We pin the true date on one of so many, don´t we Bacán!"

Preparations would begin the day before and Única would take time from where she had none to make little pointy hats out of newspaper. From her inexplicable savings she would buy candy for the children and guaro for the adults.

"Not a lot, because afterwards we have to return to work."

On the day of the birthday, Única got up earlier to heat the water and to sharpen her scissors on a pumice stone that even she did not know where she had extracted it. When Bacán awoke and noticed all the preparations, he was euphoric which compensated for all the sacrifices. But he never asked how old he was turning. He assumed that he always turned seven. The handkerchief that was tied on his head was unknotted with difficulty, and strands of his tangled hair fell across his forehead. Única undressed him and sat him down in a shallow pan. In a separate container she dissolved laundry soap from a large bag where all the detergent residues ended up after being scraped out of the discarded bags; immediately afterwards, she made a wet paste and began the task of scrubbing his entire head so that the soapy water would seep through the boy's hair and beard.

"Damn, he's already a man!"

"Momboñombo, don't be silly and don't put those ideas into him."

As she cut his locks of hair, Bacán's appearance began looking more and more like the child who was permanently fixed in Única's memory and soul. When he shed his beard, Bacán was serenely reduced to his seven years, more from his expression than from his appearance, especially after the justifiable tantrum he threw with a runny nose and tears every time the soapy water got into his eyes.

"Damn it, stop your crying. Look, Momboñombo is watching you."

And Mondolfo realized at that moment that he was witnessing unabashedly Bacán's grooming ritual, as if it were a baby's first bath. He was embarrassed but he remained there because Única begged him to stay since that was how the boy would behave better.

The soapy water ran down Bacán's hairy chest while his face was being cleaned up. The boy was playing by plunging the phone into the bucket of water and Única fought to strip off the filth adhered to his arms and legs, his neck, behind his ears, his buttocks and every inch of Bacán's body because the dump's essence was all over him, claiming him as its own property.

"*Because cleanliness, says my mother, is loveliness and keeps us healthy...*" They sang in unison at the end of that work, and Bacán looked like a newborn, rosy from the paste's scraping. A couple of hours later, his skin would return to the natural color of the dump's inhabitants, and in two weeks his beard would win back its lost territory.

Haaaaaapy Birrrrrrrrrrrrthday to you, happy birthdaaaaaaay to you, happy birrrrrrrrthday dear Bacaaaaaaan….

"Thanks to everyone and to mother Única for allowing me to turn another year old…"

For the shantytown's children this event always seemed strange. Única would unexpectedly call them together on any day, minutes before the celebration.

In the past when his birthday occurred days before Christmas, it went even better for Bacán, because around those days old toys would arrive mixed in with the rest of the trash; toys that were stranger than ever for the shantytown's children who were not up to date with transformer cars that changed from vehicles into deadly weapons for laying waste the planet; biomechanical soldiers equipped with built-in weaponry, dog robots, smart bombers… a small-scale war emerged from the bags. The adults would pick them up for Bacán not because his birthday was of any importance to them, but because a gift was equivalent to a swig of guaro at the party or a piece of candy for another child.

The dump's children became as familiar as they could with those kinds of toys by looking at them in the city's store display windows. It never crossed any child's mind that he or she might possess one.

The rest of the celebrations were set on Única's organic calendar. Her body remembered the dates that her brain had forgotten- her mother's birthday, Don Conce's and so many other dead people she paid Masses for punctually on those days toward nightfall, when Oso Carmuco would finish his labor, slip into his cassock and for better or worse, fulfill his ministry, which did not impede him from taking Llorona and relieving himself in the warmth between her legs.

"You feel so gooooood, Llorona!"

She would not answer, but the shuddering from her orgasm ended in a swarm of silent tears that Oso Carmuco would catch one by one with his tongue.

"You're always the same, Llorona, that's why we call you Llorona."

Llorona fixed her gaze on the ceiling's tin cans, naked, at times, when she would permit it, and that night she let herself be undressed slowly and she seemed somewhat consoled.

"You're not crying here for the kid... you're crying here because we both feel so good."

Oso Carmuco did not realize at what time in the early morning Llorona would automatically get up and go back to her shack. He would awaken alone on his pieces of cardboard, naked and wrapped up in his cassock and threadbare blankets as always.

In the dump dawn would arrive late, but sunsets were punctual. December hastened toward the year's inevitable decrepitude and the women divers would begin to gather together material for designing the dump's Nativity scene. Oso Carmuco helped them because he believed he was responsible for everything related to faith and traditions. Saint Joseph and the Virgin Mary were two life-sized mannequins, a man and a woman, who came to the dump years ago. Every Christmas they would arrive at the Nativity scene more damaged, because the rest of the months Oso Carmuco kept them in his shack. The man was black and the woman was a blonde Barbie, both with the attributes of their species, those that the images in churches did not possess. The woman was missing an eye; the man, an arm. The shantytown's women were not in the least amused that Oso Carmuco kept the "saints" at home, because they always came back naked at the end of the year, and they had to get them new tunics and other medieval attire so they would look like real saints. But Oso was the priest and the authority of his purple rag was more or less unquestionable.

The mannequins were placed in a little improvised stable. They put an empty cradle in the middle. Behind the cradle was a place for the ox, although there was no ox… in its place, a plastic tiger, an emblem from a former gas station, did what it could. Next to the ox went the traditional mule, but there was no mule either. A little stick pony wrapped in burlap sacks replaced it. The Baby Jesus was added on the twenty-fourth at night. That was the authentic Baby Jesus, entirely made of plaster, sporting blond curls and rosy-colored skin, like the son of a Valkyrie. Who knows what fate brought him to such an unfortunate end, but there, they honored him appropriately every December.

That year a few divers contributed a stolen cypress tree from some garden. It was large and appropriate enough to serve as a Christmas tree, to the right of the Nativity scene, decreed Oso Carmuco.

Bacán was in charge of decorating the tree… fruit cocktail cans, streamers made from toilet paper, strips of cloth and Styrofoam snow found in boxes for appliances, dolls, plastic soldiers, space ships and burned out light bulbs. And with that, Christmas was tossed away into the garbage dump.

(Singing) "Stiii-inn-kyy night."

"Oso Carmuco, that old joke is no longer appreciated by anyone, be serious!"

"Sorry doña Única…"

In chorus and with tambourines:

"Siiii-i-lent night…" etc.

One week later:

(Singing) "I will cherish the old year…"

And the old year landed in the dump with its three hundred and sixty-five days, all of them already used up because years are also thrown out when they get old.

"There's no other choice. They are either thrown out or they crush us."

"What would memory be if it could cast away dead

weight and keep only what lightens its load? Would that prevent it from capsizing at the end? Would that help it to run aground gently on some peaceful beach of death?"

"Goddamn it! Even the New Year came to the dump worn out!"

Fireworks brightened Desamparado's skies. Only the scent of burned gunpowder reached the dump.

GOVERNMENT PROMISES PERMANENT CLOSURE OF RÍO AZUL'S DUMP BY JANUARY 14th

"We're beginning the year badly… look, they say that on January 15th they're going to say where they're going to put the new dump."

Sporadic rains had fallen days before. Even the sky seemed sick of so much water and it was doing everything possible and more to vindicate itself with one or another of those orange and violet sunsets that gave one the feeling that life made sense.

The mountains looked bluer, and that hastened Mondolfo toward an empty optimism that nearly made him think it would all have a happy ending. But it was only the intoxicating effects of a suspiciously bluish sky, and something like a fresh breeze that seemed to refute the threat of methane gas that had been accumulating in the dump's bowels for some twenty years. At any moment it would explode from the most spectacular fart ever recorded in the history of indigestion.

"What a shit storm they'll make when the Government says where they're going to send all this trash!"

"Don't say shit in front of the boy! And you stop laughing, Bacán!"

"How long has it been since I smoked a cigarette… or even a cigarette butt!"

Mondolfo missed those times when he would light up a cigarette to read the newspaper. Until then he had refused second hand smoking in the dump, like Oso Carmuco and the rest of the men who had become experts in recycling old cigarettes by collecting the remaining tobacco from the cigarette butts, drying it in the sun and afterwards stuffing the sales slips in the best condition.

"I just like new cigarettes, like everyone else!"

"Then go off and smoke your mom's butt!" declared Oso Carmuco tired of so many complaints.

Activity had returned to the dump and the divers were like deranged ants; they carried loads of up to sixty times their own weight, in long rows over the slope of the hill, all secreting a musk that would guide them without any possible distraction along the path of their muted work, turning into crumbs that cake served in the center of the table… of the Meseta Central. They were indistinct but unmistakable, covered in mud; with six legs when in groups of three they would lower a large barrel of trash from a garbage truck; entering and leaving from their shacks' holes that from far away looked like just one; with long antennae when the wind flipped up their locks of hair; rolling everything around because there might always be something useful among the scraps. They were fierce and at the same time indifferent to strangers; skilled in the task of raiding the back of the garbage trucks that still had not reached the top in order to scan the cargo in them as an advantage over those who were waiting higher up. From time to time they were betrayed by their childish delight in finding some residual object from the most recent Christmas, which for an instant plucked them away from their life sentence of misery. Or when a soft drink would arrive intact and they would drink it in one gulp, proud of their find, but then violently returned to their miserable work, just like that, like ants strapped to their fate… to their unhappy fate.

The dump became dangerous during those periods of the post-Christmas hangover. Seniority was one of the selective criteria to see who would dig around first. However, a diver who was young and strong could still easily displace an old and ailing one, if the others did not defend him. There was no space even for one more soul because even the souls' intangible essence had to fight for space with the dump's malignant gases.

Única and Bacán were tied waist-to-waist with the old nylon rope, and they were diving with the certainty that the other was on each end of the rope. They were always attentive to any warning from the rope- a slight tautness meant a turn; a yank was a warning; a sudden withdrawal was an alert… but any slip-up and each one would tumble to the side with the inevitable consequence that the mother's slight frame would hit the ground until the boy noticed that he was dragging the old woman through the trash by her ass.

"Don't laugh, Bacán. Now we have to wait until he gets over his laughter…."

In twenty years nothing had changed but perhaps the most recent models of the garbage trucks… Why was anything going to change now? More than a question, it was a relief for Mondolfo who was the only one living with the anguish of hopelessness from the newspaper's reports about the dump's closure.

"What are we going to do, Única? Oh my God, what are we going to do?"

After twenty years of tolerating the dump, of watching it grow and watching it die every day the daily agony of a throbbing and feverish corpse, the residents of Río Azul, of San Antonio de Desamparados and of the surrounding areas began the new year with the firm purpose of getting rid of the dump by the end of January, at the latest. It filled their homes and their lives with its nauseating death rattle that came through the cracks in the doors, through the closed windows, through the buttonholes of their shirts and through the eyelets of their shoes. Twenty years of receiving trash that the rest of the city was sending punctually, generously, every day to their community that was no longer referred to as anything more than the dump that had taken its name.

The Government asserted that by the end of the month they would decide on a new waste site and they asked for patience. Clever Caldegueres had sent them an emotional plea that closed by saying:

"Don't ask what the country can do for Río Azul, but what Río Azul can do for the country."

And the residents, moved by the plea, ratified a new agreement until the thirtieth of April, also convinced that anything could go through life orphaned except a sanitary landfill.

It was clear that the city could not survive, not even for a week, without a forgotten place for useless things, even less if it meant the decaying specters of those things.

The garbage dump, they said, had come some twenty years ago from another community, from where it had been exiled for the same reasons that the residents of Río Azul were now alleging. At least that was the official version. In the divers' time span, ruled by other variables, the dump had always been there and there it would remain forever. If someone among them had been prepared to explain it, he or she would have said that the dump had come before the universe, or perhaps it was the oldest hell in the underworld or another more convincing mythological formula. But for them the subject was reduced simply to "this shit has always been here and no one will move it from here." And with that Mondolfo's emotions were assuaged a little.

No diver felt obliged to believe anything else. Like any person at the foot of a mountain, they experienced the ineffable smallness of their human condition with their first step uphill on the mound of clay earth, with the first roar of the garbage trucks, with the pestilent stench of decomposition, with the continuous buzzing of the flies that left no space for anything else in their heads, even though they might already be absolutely incapable of consciously perceiving it all.

Any distraction was welcome for a couple of minutes, no longer. That was why they would listen for a moment to Mondolfo's unforgivably long-winded speeches with his spiel that they had to do something. But more so because it entertained them than because of any worry over which they might lose sleep; among other things because after a full day's work, the divers' sleep had nothing in common with the warrior's rest. It was more like a small death of comfort, sinking them into the oppressive heaviness of a sleep without images, a hydraulic trash collector that devoured their soul for a few hours, and then later vomited them back into the unending day-to-day misery.

That old man is a pain in the ass!

Nonetheless, Mondolfo carefully read the newspapers and compared the information. Not a day passed without the conflict being discussed; about how each community nominated as a possible new site for that inferno, was rising up for a fight, all the residents ready to break the will of the Government. The question was always the same. "Why do we have to take on the burden of someone else's trash?" But for that question there had never been an answer. That was how you dealt with a city's sanitary landfill, or with Original Sin.

* * *

It might have been on account of the unusual cool breeze of one of those nights that chilled just a little the dump's breath of a thousand-year-old indigestion, or maybe it was the can of squid that Única found in the trash. For the first time in her life she slipped the can cleverly into the pocket of her apron, not taking it out until she was sure that Bacán would not wake up until the following day.

"Momboñombo, look at what my Guardian Angel put in a bag of trash for me!"

A can of squid! And Única had saved it to share it with him!

They sat down on the road by the shack. He pulled the easy-open tab and the can revealed its generous contents. Única brought out a pair of forks. Mondolfo had the courtesy to spear first, offering her a piece of squid to her mouth, and her stomach did a double traction flip.

In an instinctive move, she speared the evening's

second piece, and with a trembling hand repeated the gesture. He opened his mouth half way and bit down on the piece between his teeth while looking deeply into her eyes like in the movies that she had never seen nor would she ever have the chance to see and that he had already forgotten. Or like what happens to everyone when an unforeseen chemical process ignites a reaction that accepts neither excuses nor explanations. That's how they ate that damn can of squid, one little piece for her, one for him, and a small sip of ink directly from the can for each one when they finished, until only their old emaciated lips remained of the delicacy, grasping for each other with desperation like in the movies. Hell, why not! He with her face in the palm of his hand and her face trembling like a girl of sweet sixteen. Hell, why not! And their stomachs tied in knots.

"I have never been kissed…!"

And then another kiss even more voracious and her arms wrapped around his shoulders.

A cool breeze, insects trilling loudly and the light of the kerosene lamp, when there was kerosene, illuminated them a little.

He brought her to his chest and she stayed there very still, feeling something that she had given up on so long ago and now she never wanted it to end.

"Momboñombo… I…I am a virgin!"

They took each other's hands and devoured each other on Mondolfo's cardboard, where the miracle of recycled love came true. And they found the first caresses that no one had ever wanted to give them or throw away during their entire lives.

Única did not notice when Bacán had awakened, nor the moment when he rose from his cot and left the house as advised by his Guardian Buzzard.

"Oso Carmuco, OSO CARMUCOOO, I'm going to sleep here today. I think mama Única and Momboñombo are doing grown-up things."

"Sonny, it was about time they did!"

Oso Carmuco fluffed up a nice piece of cardboard for Bacán, loaned him one of his cushions, left him lying down, took his Bible and moved away to flip through it by the light of a candle.

"Única… do you want to marry me?"

"I'll speak to Oso Carmuco right away tomorrow so that he can marry us here in our neighborhood."

It had never crossed his mind that a diver might unite him in holy matrimony with the woman of his dreams.

"What the hell!"

Dawn arrived without any novelty for the rest of the world, but for the couple it dawned a little bit later than usual. After all, that would be, at best, all the honeymoon to which the future bride and groom could aspire. Undoubtedly, Única noticed that Bacán was not in his cot, but for the first time in her life, she entrusted him to the deities of the dump and curled up again.

Bacán arrived back in time for breakfast. He came

in with Oso Carmuco and they both looked slyly at the couple. They roared so loudly with laughter that you could see the holes left by his cavities, and the wired mechanism of her false teeth.

"It happened as if ordained by heaven, Oso Carmuco!"

"That's right, doña Única, since I was no longer of use in heaven, they threw me away here…"

"Even better. You are more useful here than messing around up there."

Única explained to Oso about the marriage, and between all of them they explained to Bacán what it all meant. Bacán finally understood that Mondolfo was now his dad, and he ran directly to sit on his knees and to kiss him with his coffee-soaked beard. Única joined them in the hug.

"Única, Oso Carmuco is crazy… and he's going to marry us!"

"Everyone is crazy here, haven't you realized that?"

Oso was around forty plus years old. The whole thing about the priesthood, he ended up believing it, like all the others, because his community believed it too and because he had learned the rosary by heart and even one or two of the prayers invented by Única. He was basically an alcoholic and had been on the point of sinking forever into the garbage dump of crack had Unica's will not pulled him out of that hole. "The cassock saved me," he would repeat when he was boring someone with his story; but he would say it because Única had also made him memorize it. He had a gang of friends who were not residents in the dump, who every once in a while would come for him and take him off for a good time, in spite of the protests from the women in the neighborhood. He would be lost for a couple of days, like a bear on the prowl, and he would appear unfailingly when he could go on no longer. Then he would suffer a hangover that ended in repentance and penitence, which was when he would dress in his purple cloth morning, noon, and night, compulsively flipping through his Bible as if he could concentrate on more than two words in a row of the four or five he had learned to decipher.

"He's a good boy, in spite of everything... It's those friends who lead him astray."

"He's a very nice drunk!"

"Momboñombo, you haven't learned anything. Were it not for Oso, no one would say Mass in this neighborhood."

"But Oso's Masses are ridiculous!"

"Fine, go call the priest from down below to come say Mass. The one who only goes around in a fancy car teaching any snotty kid he encounters how to drive."

"Well, let's not argue."

When mystical raptures seized him, Oso Carmuco would arm himself with a sturdy tambourine and go sing in Desamparados' garage churches. When his intoxication wore off, he would return to look for solace between Llorona's legs.

"Sometimes it's she who looks for him."

"Yes, when she's in the mood."

*   *   *

The wedding was decided for the following Monday. Nothing else was talked about in the dump, and Oso Carmuco walked around a nervous wreck trying to memorize the Wedding Mass.

Única prepared her best dress, which was not white.

"It wouldn't be correct to wear white."

Mondolfo had an impulse for an instant to come up to the surface to search for a decent suit, a good haircut, a pair of shoes, a best man and a…

He had been talking to himself for a while sitting in a clearing in the dump and observing an ant trail. He held a thin branch in his hand and from time to time he would aim and launch a fierce attack that would claim a fatality from the anthill. The rest of the ants would become disconcerted for a moment, but would then return to their deliberate tasks. A little later, one less ant in the world! He was doing it distractedly, without malice, without enjoying the insects' misfortune, instead with an enormous indifference, until the idea hit him in the gut that this must be what death is like, that with the same indifference, God would simply point one by one at the victims of the human anthill and that's how they would fall down dead, before the consternation of the rest, who at the end of a short while had no other alternative but to continue in the line. He made the sign of the cross and decided not to go out looking for any of those things that he would not find anyway beyond the dump, where he had found all the other indispensable things for his wedding: a bride, a son, and a couple of friends.

"Única, we could tell the Novios to take advantage of this moment and get married in the same Mass with us!"

"The Novios are already married. Did you forget that already?"

Between a few divers and the attendant at the entrance to the dump, they hammered together a kind of altar from where Oso Carmuco would give it his all.

That morning in the middle of the dump the personnel suspended the trash collection and the residents from San José thought that a new strike was going on. The women helped to prepare Única. After a good soak, they unbraided her hair and made up her face the best they could. Única had taken care of Bacán´s preparations the night before.

The attendant at the entrance, a friend of Mondolfo´s from his very first days, arrived with a surprise. He lent the groom his entire suit with everything from the tie to the black buckled shoes. It was a blue suit more for a first communion than for a wedding, but who would care about that? In addition, the good man brought a white suit from one of his sons, which fit Bacán fabulously: short pants that showed the fuzzy hair on his skinny legs, short-sleeved shirt, and white shoes.

"He looks like a little angel!"

"The whole thing was botched. Oso Carmuco came down with the runs from an attack of nerves! Tomorrow, without fail."

The residents of the neighborhoods who would put out their refuse on Tuesdays, thought the same thing that day as those who do it on Mondays, because at first light the dump was already set to celebrate the first wedding in the history of the country, celebrated in a dump with only elements native to that place.

Oso Carmuco was on his feet at four thirty in the morning, trembling with cold and with the fear that he would lose his nerve again. He had heard confession and had absolved almost everybody in the dump; he had said Midnight Mass several years in a row and he had almost given last rites to Mondolfo; but he had never performed a marriage for anyone.

Don Retana, the oldest diver in the community, gave the bride away. The groom received her at the altar. Those in attendance were shouting: "you can do it, you can do it!" Bacán marched with the rings on a small plate; don Retana had given them as a wedding gift the rings that he had once used at his own wedding, which were the entirety of all the assets he possessed.

The Mass began with a "Please rise." The attendees were already standing and they let the priest know it with whistles and shouts of laughter. So, Oso raised his hands ceremoniously and said, "Then sit." But since there was nowhere to sit, they whistled at him again.

Oso began to get nervous, but the old man and woman were so happy they were also laughing with the guests.

"We are gathered together here… how does it go? … to unite this man with this woman in holy matrimony."

Oso Carmuco digressed for a good while over biblical themes. He spoke about Earthly Paradise and he gave assurance that it existed in San Francisco de Dos Ríos. He spoke about the Three Wise Kings and said that he knew them. He spoke about the Eucharist and said that she was a very nice woman.

He finally landed on the customary, "Do you take this woman to be your lawful wife, bla, bla, bla."

"You don't say bla, bla, bla, damn it, you say: to protect her and to honor her until death do you part!"

"Sorry, Momboñombo."

And the dump's community broke out into applause, some threw trash up in the air, they shouted and they whistled, and Oso Carmuco sang a folk song:

"Twooooooo heaaaaaaaaats were joined, they are joined, they will jooooooin haaaaands."

And the divers ate, drank and sang, and for a good part of the morning they forgot that happiness has a bar code.

Bacán played with the other children, ran around the guests, frightened away the buzzards by throwing stones at them and cried when his mother scolded him for mistreating animals.

Única was very moved during the ceremony. She thought about her mother.

That day was the second happiest of her life.

A squadron of police officers who arrived to investigate why the gates to the dump were closed abruptly interrupted the party. It was explained to them that there was a wedding, but, in their most official fashion, "move along, move along," they ended the celebration and forced them to open the gates to the long line of garbage trucks waiting outside.

Everything returned to normal.

The following day the municipal workers from garbage collection began to strike. The strike was announced months earlier as a result of the just cause that at least ten new units were needed to cope with the collection.

* * *

It was a long week of strikes.

The city streets were neatly crammed with trash, and the dump was bellowing for its food.

Passersby were disconcerted.

A bitter scent came from San José's stagnant air. Dogs, cats, rats, flies, and who knows what other kinds of urban creepy crawlies were ripping open the bags and strewing the garbage along the sidewalks.

The divers were perplexed. The trash had left the dump as if the sea had suddenly abandoned its beach of a thousand years.

If the trash is not going to the dump, the divers are going to the trash: brigades of divers swarmed the streets of San José. But a diver on the city streets is like a sailor on land- he gets dizzy, and becomes disoriented.

Linear streets, straight-lined sidewalks- a feeling of infinitude overwhelmed the divers and intimidated them. A networking of streets without any meaning that did not inspire any principle of order. They were crossing from one sidewalk to another without paying any attention to the cars, which inevitably were braking sharply and blowing their horns forcefully at them, but the divers scarcely noticed. They would come and go along the same block, often without realizing that they had already passed by there, and not because they weren't acquainted with the city, because not a one of them had ever gotten lost, but because it was one thing to walk there during their free time and another thing to go out to work in an unfamiliar environment.

Buzzards hovered very low over the streets of the city.

Pages from the newspapers testified to the crisis: full-colored photographs that looked like archival prints of pedestrians holding their noses, jumping over a pile of rubbish, protesting on camera; the news broadcasts already had enough material to make a full-length movie, between interviews with President Caldegueres, with legislators, with Secretaries, with the residents from the neighborhoods and hundreds of images taken at a prudent distance from the divers fully practicing their profession.

In one week the dump had inundated San José and threatened to stay. Tons of trash, our trash! Rolling around the streets...

What will the tourists think!

On the fourth day of the strike, the Municipality of San José "initiated actions," as one says in journalese, in the presence of other councils and the Department of Public Works and Transportation to "put into effect an emergency plan:" two thousand metric tons of trash were on the streets and the residents from all the neighborhoods continued to bring even more bags several times a day.

The Greater Metropolitan Area, "The GMA," in newspaper language, could already hear the stomping of the plague's great beast. *"If dead rats begin to appear, we'll place the blame on Camus,"* exclaimed witty Caldegueres, and the witticism was celebrated as usual, and commented upon in the newspapers in the section, "The Latest from don Junior María."

Some of the owners of commercial establishments opted to hire privately owned collection services in order to get rid of their trash. That strategy was somewhat successful and it even served as an argument for endorsing the proposal for the privatization of the dump.

What was never stated was where in the hell did they take the collected trash… What did they do with it…? That remained a mystery.

On Friday the strike came to a happy end. The Municipality of San José requested help from the other municipalities and that night, with workers and borrowed trucks, under the supervision of law enforcement, they collected several tons of waste. On Saturday, around noon, everyone had already forgotten about the strike, about the trash in the streets, about the pestilence in the air, and about the divers walking along the sidewalks and running into everyone. For the comfort and health of the citizens, the sea of trash returned to the beaches of Río Azul. The fetid liquids dropped to levels of tolerance and the city returned to its frightful routine.

The return of the trash collectors deeply affected the dump. A week of hunger had left the landfill in a terrible mood, groaning and trembling from fever and rage.

Those on board were coming to the end of their reserves when they spied the line of trucks from the foot of the hill up to the highest point. They came out to receive them like prodigal sons. The tractors led the procession. The noise returned to the relief of the divers. Even Mondolfo felt happy and optimistic.

Amongst the backlog of newspapers came the news that the Government was studying fourteen possible locations for the new landfill; sites "offered by individuals and other entities." There were fourteen finalists in the big pageant.

The first community called to the stage was Miss Orotina, who modeled a daring suit of tear gas when the anti-riot police confronted some one thousand five hundred residents disarmed to the teeth, who blockaded, in peaceful protest, the main highway, certain points along the highway to Quepos, and positioned their buses in Cuatro Esquinas and Pozón de Coyolar.

"A garbage dump in Orotina… In exchange for what?"

Part of the Government's plan was to put tons of trash from the GMA onto trains so that it would travel from the Station of the Pacific to the new place of its eternal rest.

The tear gas forced the residents to take refuge in a lounge on the edge of the highway. The Civic Committee Against the Installation of a Landfill in Orotina, and the local priest reported to the press that the residents had been beaten and gassed by the police officers, to whom they had offered sandwiches and soft drinks as proof of their nonviolent position.

In spite of the televised images of the Red Cross assisting women, children and the elderly, victims of the tear gas, and men who were victims of the beatings, the Government asserted that it would take more drastic measures against the insurgents, "whose position was irrational and incomprehensible."

Orotina was ready to wage war.

The Government declared that it would consider other possibilities.

Orotina lowered the alarm from red to orange.

The uncertainty kept the country in suspense.

Here and there someone would make a statement in favor of the transportation of trash by railroad, until the Secretary of Health declared that the garbage dump would be installed in a community, which up to that point had not been announced.

* * *

The finalists spent an entire week with their hearts in their throats. Miss Orotina, the favorite of the panel of judges, Miss Uruca, Miss Turrúcares, Miss Atenas as Miss Photogenic, and a number of other young ladies. But it wasn't until the beginning of the following week that Miss Esparza came out dumbfounded in the photo, when, by decree, the Government selected her as Miss New Sanitary Landfill. Tears, applause, parading down the runway...

Around seven o'clock in the evening, one thousand five hundred residents from Esparza were on the Inter-American Highway taking part in a blockade, as the police force was transferring a contingent of eight hundred anti-riot officers, those who hate soft drinks and sandwiches.

The Government was not willing to tolerate any interruption of flow on the highway, "because it threatens the citizens' rights to move freely."

The news broadcasts for their part continued to urge Esparza's inhabitants "to abandon that selfish stance." But the site had been chosen with no criterion except for the fact that it was somewhat remote, a mile or so from populated areas.

There was no study on the environmental impact. Caldegueres announced: "The study has not been carried out yet but it will give positive results…"

"You see Momboñombo, there is a study, but it's not done yet!"

The newspapers gave up generous space to the news on Esparza.

Violence erupted. Tear gas, beatings, blows- and a water pump tank which six months before had still been sleeping the sleep of the just in a corner of the International Airport, now making its triumphal entrance through the streets of the city.

Esparza panicked. The tank was a donation from the Gringo Government some twenty years ago. Who would have thought it! The tank had performed emergency services for ten years in the airport's Fire Department and had been taken out of circulation as junk. But the eagle eye of one police officer discovered it, inspired by a television program on police heroes. The Government said, "Tank, get up and go." And after an investment of sixteen million pesos to repair it, to reconstruct the eight-cylinder diesel engine, the automatic transmission, the cabin and its water cannon that would shoot water at four hundred and fifty pounds of pressure, the tank was ready for any would-be Rambo who might drive it.

The tank with its pump unit went in accompanied by a tanker truck that would alleviate the tank's thirst after every two thousand liters of water discharged.

Eight minutes later the highway was cleared. The residents fled, soaked, hurt, humiliated and offended, poisoned by the gases, beaten by the police, filmed by the press… The tank´s water pump shot water left and right and posed for the cameras… it looked so manly…

The police helicopter loosened the roofs of Esparza's houses, and the tank paraded down the streets shooting water every so often, breaking shop windows, loosening wood walls, drenching people, imposing order, protecting justice, defending democracy, freedom of transit and the civil rights of businessmen who were competing to take over the dump once it was privatized.

Esparza's residents attempted legal channels by filing a Writ of Protection before the Fourth Penal Court; they warned that if the Government did not set aside the decree, more blood would be shed… the residents' blood, of course.

The Government had already awarded the construction of the new landfill to a foreign company. Of course! And to stimulate healthy competitiveness, they even considered a proposal from a local micro-business owner who wanted to offer private services for trash collection in his own vehicle to whoever might want to hire him. The case remained in the state of "let's see;" in the meantime the foreign company was initiating steps to begin the project's viability studies announcing that it was ready to invest initially somewhere between four and five million dollars in the construction of a landfill with a useful lifespan of nearly thirty years for the benefit of San Jose's thirteen counties and Cartago's four.

* * *

Dazed by the pressure from the sea of waste, the divers worked mechanically against that heavy mass.

Moving from one place to another required an effort to dig out their feet sunken up to their ankles in sludge, and moving their legs that were bogged down up to their knees in trash. Each stroke of their arms also had to move the weight of the bags they used to take the treasures rescued from the depths. Fainting caused by a lack of oxygen could turn into a fatal accident; a tractor might pass over a human body without the driver noticing. One careless mistake and the jagged mouth of the power shovels would turn into a shark's bite, which could bring with it one arm or one leg less. A deep current was capable of dragging a child down and swallowing him forever, like Llorona's child. Running into a rat's nest was like falling into a well of carnivorous fish, and more than one diver had lost toes by diving barefoot in those infested waters.

In spite of so many pitfalls on the road to their daily bread, the divers worked mechanically as if in their heads no activity of any kind was occurring.

"Sometimes time gets away from me without my thinking about anything!"

Mondolfo would become panicked when he realized that he had spent half a morning without remembering anything, without images in his head, without ideas, and even without agony. It filled him with fear, sometimes a great deal of fear, because it was like suddenly seeing himself in a stranger´s body.

Everyone worked that way in the dump. Almost everyone would strike up long and incomprehensible monologues bent over the trash, and that was how they also behaved in the city. But there on the wave of asphalt it was easy to distinguish the diver from the beggar: the beggar, sitting in his rags, raises his hand automatically with the palm side up. The diver, in his interminable walking, every once in a while lowers his hand with the palm side down, his fingers ready to grab objects that are immediately subjected to an evaluation by his senses. They smell them, they taste them, they shake them to see if something rattles inside; and only then do they subject them to the criterion of their eyes if none of the previous senses produce positive results. If their eyes also fail to decipher the object's usefulness, then they turn to a higher court ruling: the diver tries to imagine what benefit the thing he found could bring him. However, when he arrives at that stage, generally the object is returned to the streets from where it was about to be rescued. The beggar's gaze is directed at the person to whom he addresses his pleading. The diver's gaze is connected to his hands, even more so to his fingers. Nevertheless they look so much alike, both reduced to parasitic organisms in society´s digestive system, except that one is a root system passively waiting for the arrival of some nourishment, while the other is a carnivorous plant- generating and emitting the aroma that attracts prey, and taking what people discard without asking.

Mondolfo was not able to formulate it in this way. He only felt that he was hatching perhaps his last ideas before falling entirely into the divers' unconsciousness; that little by little his memories would be fading away from him; that his relationship with Única, who had literally saved his life, would become blurred in the depths of that dead sea from the lack of any damn hope. That he would end his life diving like an absurd machine only to stay alive purely due to the habit of being alive and not because he might hope for something more.

"I am an old man… But there are so many young people here!"

The Novios might have a couple of months more than he living off the trash. But one day in hell is a century in the dump, and by that time, they were already looking at each other as if they were strangers, he at her, she at him. They were together to share the worse, the poorer and the sickness until death do they part, like the priest had made them swear the day of their wedding, only to forget them immediately and forever.

In the midst of that vile routine, the Novios were already looking at one another with disgust. They were fully aware that neither of them was at fault. They would repeat angrily to each other that poverty is not the fault of the poor, but resentment had already seized their souls and had dried up their hearts.

Mondolfo had spent more than one half hour paralyzed, seeing everything as blurry images, as if he were seeing the rest of his life in the glass of the premonitory bottle he held in his hand. What was left of his life was to dive with his mind gone blank, with his five senses heightened, with one in each finger to be able to think with a hand that had learned to see with rat eyes, to smell with a buzzard´s sense of smell, to taste with a fly's tongue, to hear like a dog and to feel like... like... That was the shitty part! He couldn't stop feeling like a human being. And up there, in his head, the day-by-day misery had taught him to disconnect his ears from the ignition of the tractors' motors; the dump's vapors had closed down his sense of smell; the recycled food had sealed off his sense of taste; the gasses from decomposition were eating away at his sleeping eyes open in that zombie's wakeful state. And the filth on his skin was separating him from the world with a sticky film that was the authentic skin of extreme poverty.

Only toward evening, at the end of a day's work, would Mondolfo's consciousness return to him with great difficulty, when his family demanded his attention. Then it would return to him like flashes of light... that was his life, he had not died, nor had he spent even five months as a resident of hell. That was his life.

"Let's get out of here!"

"What did you say?"

"Let's get out of this hell."

"Did you go crazy again?"

"No! I am speaking seriously. If we don't leave, then we *will* go crazy. Besides, they're going to throw us out of here anyway."

* * *

A cold front fell over the region. Fifty-five degrees in the early mornings of February could kill anyone who did not have a decent roof over decent walls of the precarious human condition.

"Cold in February, Única. What in the world is God thinking?"

"Don't bring God into this."

Bacán's cough was close to ripping him apart, and the old man and woman did not close their eyes the entire night trying to warm his chest, rubbing it with alcohol until the bottle ran out, and then they used bottles of perfume, rancid ointments and old balms that Única would pick up. But the boy only managed to sleep when they warmed his chest with a rubber pouch to keep the water hot, almost boiling. The water bottle had arrived at the dump without a top, of course. Mondolfo would light the fire and heat the water, and Única came up with a way to close the mouth of the pouch with a cork stopper wrapped in plastic, then secured with elastic bands or shoe laces or whatever would hold it in place. However, when none of those precautions prevented the hot water from spilling over the boy's right shoulder, from that moment on they would have to wait until he was very tired before he would allow them to put it on him.

"Única, this boy should be seen by a doctor…"

The following day was foul weather. Bacán stayed home convalescing and his parents went out to work exhausted from lack of sleep.

"What must God be thinking?"

"Don't bring God into this."

"It doesn't matter. God won't get involved, anyway."

"If you continue blaspheming, I'm going to get a divorce."

"There are no lawyers here…"

"The pain in my legs is killing me. The cold always does that to me."

Halfway through the morning, the old man and woman took a break to go see Bacán, to prepare him a hot drink and to spend a little time with him.

"This boy is turning yellow."

"That's how he gets with the flu."

The divers would keep themselves warm with whatever they could, but it was never sufficient. Some would come out wrapped in burlap sacks that they used as blankets, but the cold wind seeped through everywhere. The grey sky was a landfill of clouds used up in the north and dragged to their country by the winds' garbage truck.

Oso Carmuco went out to work with the purple cassock, and without his knowing it he infused a kind of courage into the community, watching their priest working without privileges and enduring with them God's graces.

The divers lit bonfires in large barrels and the attendant threatened to call the police if they did not put them out, because a fire in the great dump of Río Azul could provoke a serious explosion of methane gas. But the divers did not understand what that was, nor did they believe that such a thing was possible. However, they obeyed from pure fear thinking that the police might come to explain it to them.

In the city the same cold wind was blowing for its consumers; also divers, but from other seas, with other pursuits and other kinds of suffering that would simply be incomprehensible to any of the dump's inhabitants, their complete opposites.

The wind was carrying February away, and what a couple of months before would have been a relief to Mondolfo's nose and lungs, at this stage in his life it wasn't anything more than a hellish cold because he could no longer make a distinction between fresh air and the dump's putrid exhalations.

The cold front's nights turned the shacks into freezers. The tin cans on the roof and on the walls grew cold to the point of keeping the desolation of those on board from becoming spoiled.

"I even miss October's rain storms. At least it wasn't so cold!"

* * *

The dump's closure became news again, but this time to initiate a new schedule. The President declared that the new landfill would begin operating on the first of June and that Río Azul's residents must wait until April thirtieth for the closure of the dump, without blocking streets, without protests, without bellowing. Nevertheless, the presidential promise, true to his nature, was completely without foundation. The land's soil treatment at Cabezas de Esparza would be any fucking day around three o'clock; the adaptation of the train for transporting the trash, a little later, and the repairs to the railway lines would conclude the following day.

Some talking heads spoke about systematic recycling as the only alternative to the trash problem: an obligatory sorting of the waste; trash bags, public dumps and garbage collectors for different kinds of waste; even-numbered days for organic waste, odd-numbered days for solid wastes, etc. To fully inculcate this kind of discipline in the country's entire population would require a project that would last at least two generations. Meanwhile, the trash would already have taken over a good part of the national territory; and the grotesque number was not an unfortunate exaggeration. In fact, the networking between the river basins of the GMA already looked like gigantic open cut sewers. The María Aguilar, Torres, Tiribí, Segundo, Grande, Ocloro and Tártoles rivers and the Lentisco, Negritos, Bermúdez and Rivera streams were choking between the waters coming from the commercial coffee mills, everyone's shit and the chemical waste from more than a few factories.

In short, the entire country suffered the fate of the towns that did not know what to do with their trash: it had turned into an enormous trash heap and there was not a single inhabitant who could brag about not having some element of a diver in the innermost of his or her heart. For many years now there was no one who did not dive in the air, in the waters and in the contaminated food because there is so much junk food now and still more to come... chemicals, agrichemicals, pesticides, sewage and the rest of the aromatic herbs, of which no one keeps count any longer.

* * *

If old Mondolfo had known that more than ten years later the dump would still be there where he had found it, he surely would not have taken the trouble trying to decipher the information from the newspapers, nor would his soul have been tormented thinking about his family's future. But the old man divided his time between work and the soap opera that had become the dump's closure and the opening of the landfill.

An early senility was taking over him. Even the divers' attention was drawn to the way he was speaking to himself, how long his beard had grown, and how bulging his eyes had become.

"If you continue in this way, we'll soon be burying you."

His hair was falling out in fistfuls.

"Pretty soon I'm going to need a wig."

Mondolfo's body had been withering away during those months that he spent in the shantytown, which he counted on each new hole that he made on his pant belt. His body's silent protest oscillated between rage and resignation, but in the end his rage always won.

The old man had the most outlandish idea of all his ideas up to that moment: he armed himself with paper and pencil, which were not lacking in Única's house owing to the habits from her former profession, not because they served any purpose; and he sat down to write a letter to the President of the Republic.

"Dear Junior María Caldegueres…"

Who knows what things he scribbled in the hours that it took for him to fill up two sheets of paper, which he came out to show everyone as if he carried under his arm the Declaration of Human Rights.

The old man was filled with a happiness that seemed to have been recently thrown into the trash only for him.

"I tell him everything here, Única, everything! I tell him that I met his father in the days of the revolution. I tell him about you, about Bacán, about Oso Carmuco, about all of us who live here…"

"How disgraceful, Momboñombo!"

"It's a disgrace to rob from the poor. Look, I'm telling him to help us look for a job, that we are humble people, that…"

"And you know how to write all that?"

"Well, one does what one can do…" the old man said proudly showing her the letter. "I tell him that we poor people are not bad…"

"That paper is so old. I've had it since I came to live here…"

"This time he will surely pay attention to me."

The following day, don Mondolfo Moya Garro awoke with the spirit of a go-getter. He rose from his bed humming songs from his youth; he brushed his teeth, and said that he was going out to run an errand.

At the guard post he did not stop for more than a second to say hello. He walked running his hand along the school patio's chain-link fence, saying hello to the children who did not even turn to look at him.

He came to the stop for the San Francisco-Río Azul bus, he took out a couple of coins extracted from Única´s "little box," and he waited the obligatory forty-five minutes until the dilapidated old bus appeared that serviced the community. Once on board he did not notice the other passengers' repugnant stares; the old man sat in the first seat with the intention of speaking to the driver.

"Grandpa, quiet down, or you get off now!"

"They were friendlier before." He was about to respond to him, but the fear that he would be asked to get off half way to his stop led to prudence and he remained silent.

A noise slipped through the funnel of his ears, and it took awhile for him to realize that it was music…music! Music still existed. He had not heard it since his arrival to the shantytown… His eyes grew moist.

"A great bolero from my time!" As if time had ever been his.

The trip to downtown San Francisco seemed like an eternity to him. He got off at the bypass route's stop, waited the obligatory half hour until the vehicle appeared that took him, at the risk of his own life, to Zapote, the seat of the Presidential House. He got off and walked very slowly, as if tractors were turning over his guts, until he arrived at the gates of the building.

A group of heavily armed police officers were in the

reception area.

"Good morning…"

There was no response.

"Good morning…"

Again, there was no response.

"Pardon me if I am bothering you, gentlemen."

Harsh glances were directed at the old man.

"You see I have brought a very important letter for don Junior María."

Bursts of laughter.

Another attempt to make himself understood.

More bursts of laughter.

Anguish.

Indifference.

"Sirs, this is very serious…"

The entire morning would have continued in this way had the police officers' patience not worn thin. One of them accepted the grimy piece of paper from the old man's hands and promised him that he would deliver it personally to the Republic's Head of State.

Mondolfo, very confused, but still optimistic, set out on the return trip home.

"On foot!"

The price of a fare was exorbitant for a diver.

A couple of hours later he was home again, where he found an inconsolable Única because her husband had abandoned her…

"You want to drive me crazy!"

She had spent the entire morning thinking the worst; but when he told her about the delivery of the letter, she forgave him from the damn pity she felt for him.

"Caldegueres is going to respond to us soon. I am certain."

Mondolfo's bold move caused a profound although ephemeral impact among those on board.

"That man over there, believe it or not, you don't want to mess with him."

That day, the old man dug into the trash as if he were farming the land.

Única spoke seriously to him…

"Now that you have already gone to deliver the letter, promise me that you're going to calm down, and that you're going to stop walking around here with a silly look on your face only thinking about misfortunes."

He agreed. He was certain that the answer would not take more than a month to arrive.

* * *

From the cold wave of February, without any spring-like transition, it went straight to March's sweltering heat.

Bacán had scarcely recovered from his illness. He had become thin and sallow, weak, "half-hearted" they said.

Keeping Bacán out of earshot, Única told her husband how during a cold front like the one that had just gone by, in that circumstance, and without anyone noticing until several days later, an elderly woman, a neighbor on the side of the dump facing the highway, had died a strange death.

The elderly woman knew that something was happening to her in her legs, or in some place, because each time it was more difficult for her to move any part of her body.

"Maybe I got lucky and I'm dying…" she was heard saying when she climbed from the base of the bridge to the highway, or when she came down with her bag almost empty from what the day's work had given her. That's why those from under the bridge decided to move her shack up to the side of the highway.

They did it because it was shameful to see an elderly woman going up and down the hill with a sack of ailments and an empty bag. She was too old for that sort of thing, and she was alone.

From the bottom of her heart she was thankful for what they did.

"On what side should we put your house?"

"Looking toward the highway!" she said without letting pass the first and last opportunity in her life to ask for something pleasurable.

With her house scarcely a few yards from the highway's East-West traffic lane, it was enough for her to leave the door open to entertain herself watching the streaks of color that the automobiles left in their wake. When the door was closed, at night, the purring of the motors helped her to fall asleep.

Up above, she recognized the old faithful cold: she awoke with her feet frozen stiff and her nose moist, like when she was living at the base of the bridge.

One night, out of the clear blue sky, a bit of heat began to warm her feet. She curled up between her burlap sacks without waking up, and she spent the coziest morning that she had not had in years.

She awakened much later than was customary and enjoyed a good while longer that inexplicable miracle, until she started the painful ritual of lifting her body, which had nothing more to give. When she succeeded in sitting up, she lowered her gaze…she stayed motionless. When her fear passed, she laughed about the miracle. A fox had given birth in the burlap sacks, exactly between her feet, and with a mother's zeal, the fox was nursing her six babies, and growling at the woman each time she perceived the slightest movement.

In a few days, someone let it be known that the old woman had not been seen for quite some time. They found her rigid, with her eyes fixed on the baby foxes. The fox was not there, but she arrived before long… The motors were purring along unfazed scarcely a few yards from the door.

* * *

March's heat began to rip apart the dump's surface. A web of crevices allowed gases to escape from the subsoil.

Mondolfo was sadly pleased that his sense of smell was still capable of detecting something. Of course, it wasn't what he would have wanted. It seemed as if suddenly everything would melt, with the buzzards floating like oil slicks on the sea of trash that would cascade down after a sudden thaw, sweeping away the entire country in its wake.

"Damn heat. I really prefer the rain!"

"You're never happy. Isn't that right, Momboñombo?"

All the rotting stuff that came to the dump sped up its decaying process, which left the divers with enormous losses.

The flies were reproducing endlessly and the film of dirt on the divers' skin was cracking like the ground.

During that time of year, the age-old punishment of thirst fell over the dump's community with greater viciousness than that of hunger.

The divers pieced together tents of a sort with their burlap sacks to protect themselves from sun exposure whenever they could. Not even Única's commanding tone could make Oso Carmuco put on his old purple rag.

"A priest does not go around without a shirt, or in short pants, no matter how hot it is!"

The top of the hill was like a cauldron. It would not cool down, even at night, so the divers came out to sleep under the open sky because the zinc cans on their roofs and walls were turning into a brutal oven.

The desperation for water scattered the community

throughout nearby neighborhoods. When they could, the divers would drink directly from the garden faucets and afterwards, they would fill their buckets and flee. The operation was more effective late at night, when people were sleeping and did not hear the water thieves and did not go out to chase them away. Some neighbors took off the wing nut from the faucet to avoid the theft. However, the divers usually came armed with their own emergency wing nuts.

"No one should deny anyone a little bit of water...!"

"Well, now you see. We don't even have the right to that!"

"When the President looks for jobs for us, we are going to buy a little house, with a garden and everything..."

"What are you talking about?"

"Well, about the letter, when the President reads it, he's going to help us and..."

March, perishable and biodegradable, reached the average life span for any month, and died in the dump, leaving its unfinished tasks to April. The usual multitude of divers attended the burial; a procession of more than one hundred trash collector hearses, and the buzzards dressed in deep mourning for a life spent in sorrow.

And the new month made its triumphal entrance under a terrifying headline:

RÍO AZUL WILL CLOSE
THE LANDFILL ON APRIL 30th

"The answer to the letter did not arrive… Who would have thought it?"

"It was the guards. They did not give the letter to don Junior María, because if they had given it to him…"

"And if they did give it to him? Could it be that you put some vulgar remark in the letter and you offended the President?"

In April the heat began to ease up a bit.

"The previous presidents would go out to speak to the people."

"What presidents are you talking about?"

"About the ones before…"

"And haven't you thought that maybe Caldegueres did read your letter but he refused to answer you?"

"Do you really believe that he would do such a thing? If one day he would come to speak to the poor… if he saw how we live, if he knew the hardships we suffer…"

Única did not have the courage to reveal her conviction to him that Mr. President really had been notified of the letter. And, in effect, he had found out something about "a piece of paper that a beggar left for him," as the police officers' account stated. They had delivered it to him thinking that it would make him laugh. However, that kind of evidence of poverty in the country did not amuse the Head of State. Each time he saw a poor person, he would deliver the same old tirade that they were not poor, that the poor made themselves. Because if anyone could get mashed taro root to eat, there was no reason to feel poor; just as he had let the people know in one of his famous Presidential messages in which he made an effort to bring common sense to the people by advising them to renounce superfluous knowledge leftover from an obsolete educational system.

"Mathematics... For what?" the self-named "Wise Bull" would say in his effort to guide the national horde, consolidated into a single political bandwagon after the very famous "Caldegueres Pact" that he signed with himself.

"When has someone's life improved because he or she knew by heart the capitals of the world?" he proclaimed emotionally, racking his brain in search of the best way to explain himself before a citizenry that, in his judgment, thought with the logic of the mentally disabled.

"What is the purpose of violins without entrepreneurs?" he would proclaim solemnly, urging sculptors to erect statues honoring the members of the House of Commerce and poets to sing about their distinguished records.

"Citizens that represent us in international programs is what this country needs," affirmed Big Brother closing his fist as if he were squeezing a silicone ball.

The grubby piece of paper with don Mondolfo Moya

Garro's scribbling flapped in his hand. He crumpled it and deposited it personally into his office wastebasket without even glancing at it, thus closing the case of the beggar.

* * *

And in April the end of the world began. It was all accomplished. The landfill would close its doors forever on the thirtieth at three o'clock in the afternoon, or the residents of Río Azul would close it by force, and they would block the garbage trucks' access.

Satisfied as per the agreement with the Government, the neighboring communities washed their hands of the matter; going forward the tons of trash that the GMA produced daily would never again be their problem.

The document had been signed by the Presidential Secretaries, of National Resources, of Energy and Mines, and of National Security. It established that failure to comply with any of the points stipulated in the document would be cause for the cancellation of that agreement, releasing the affected party from all responsibility.

Nonetheless, the President's Chief of Staff made it publicly known that the agreement signed with the residents would be submitted to a Council of Notables for further study in order to ascertain any possible anomalies.

The news fell like a missile throughout the communities. The leaders endorsed the intention of those represented of finalizing the matter according to what was signed and the Secretary of National Security threatened to use the police force if the residents were "to infringe on public rights" like freedom of transit, surely thinking about the garbage trucks' freedom of transit...

"The Government only deceives us…"

"The Government deceives everyone…"

The entire country was fully abreast of the Government's inability to find a solution to the trash problem. It was simple. There was no place to dump it. However, a few days later, it was announced that the foreign company, in charge of the construction of the new landfill, had now concluded the environmental impact studies on Esparza's land. The facts generated by the study were surprising: the site was so favorable for constructing a new dump there that no one could explain how God had not designated it for such purposes from the moment of the Creation of the World.

For their part, the University's scientists had carried out their studies in the area and their conclusions were spectacularly different: the landfill would be located as far away from the city as no other in the world, which would substantially increase the costs of the garbage collection for the general public. In addition, it would gravely affect the zone´s ecological equilibrium and its surrounding areas, the tourism interests in several communities and an infinite number of inconveniences.

The results had been political, not scientific, which

was why the Government insisted on maintaining that designation.

If Mondolfo Moya Garro had known that the GMA's trash would never end up in Esparza, he would not have despaired so much, nor would he have devised the pressure tactic that he proposed to the more than four hundred divers in the shantytown. A Peace March!

"Of course, to the Presidential House!"

He spoke with everyone. He looked for them one by one and he explained the situation to them. He went from shack to shack and he spoke for days on end during the dinner hour. He talked, and talked, and talked...

"That's for sure; everyone will do a good job brushing their teeth before going to speak to the President."

Única was a sensible woman, an enemy to all brash actions. She was not completely won over by the idea.

"You're also going to take me to speak to the President?"

"Of course, Bacán. If we didn´t, whom would be leave you with?"

Oso Carmuco promised to wear his cassock that day.

The old man walked around with yellowed newspapers that he used as his arguments for convincing the ones on board to stop earning their bread on that day in order to walk a couple of miles.

"He's a strange man!"

"But he says it´s so they won't run us off from here."

Única was feeling nervous about the march. Her

fellow women divers were asking her if she would go…

"If you are going, I am going…"

There might have been around fifty divers who were convinced when Mondolfo announced the march for the following day.

The instructions were simple: everyone must behave well, not a rock, not a curse word. Everyone had to shake Mr. President's hand and greet him politely.

And dressed in their finest clothes, fifty or so divers formed a line and went down the hill in the direction of the Presidential House.

There were women divers with their children divers, men divers, old divers, and a dog or two that joined them at different stretches along the march. Ordinary people were watching the implausible spectacle of that march, like medieval lepers who were interrupting traffic and infringing upon the drivers' freedom of movement. Oso Carmuco was dancing merrily like one of those giant clowns, with his head to one side and his arms dangling limply, and the divers were happy in their naiveté singing "The Sea Was Serene."

The chorus:

"With an A. Tha saa waaas sarane, sarane waaas tha saa, tha saa waaas saraaane, sarane waaas tha saa."

Don Mondolfo Moya Garro led the march. Very few times in his life had he been so happy, so sure of having found the solution to a problem.

The chorus:

"With an E. Thee seee weees sereeene, sereeene weees thee seee, thee seee weees sereeene, sereeene weees thee seee."

Única was leading Bacán by the hand and he was greeting people as he went by.

Llorona did not know in what they had involved her, but she was trudging along with her doll on her back and with her lost stare at Única's side.

The chorus:

"With an I. Thi siii wiiis siriiine, siriiine wiiis thi siii, thi siii wiiis siriiine, siriiine wiiis thi siii."

Nobody understood what was happening. The drivers were growing furious, blowing their horns. The pedestrians were stopping to watch the parade of discarded people pass by and more than one person thought they were actors who were disturbing the peace just for fun.

The chorus:

"With an O. Tho sooo wooos sorooone, sorooone wooos tho sooo, tho sooo wooos sorooone, sorooone wooos tho sooo."

The blight of poverty descended and passed through San Antonio de Desamparados, crowded into San Francisco de Dos Ríos and threatened to arrive at Zapote by midday, because when misery accumulates and reaches its threshold, you only have to wait for it to spill over the rest of society.

The chorus:

"With a U. Thu suuu wuuus suruuune, suruuune wuuus thu suuu, thu suuu wuuus suruuune, suruuune wuuus thu suuu."

Along the way, more divers joined them without asking where they were going, nor their purpose.

As a precaution, people let them pass and the drivers suppressed their desire to run over them. The owners of the commercial establishments with doors facing the street ordered them to be closed while the extraordinary parade was passing by. However, one and a half miles or so from their goal, a patrol car reached them and went to the head of the parade where they interrogated Mondolfo.

"Yes, to speak to the President."

The police officers saw a group of people dressed in rags. They saw the determination of their leader to carry on until the ultimate consequences, and true to their instincts, the guardians of order reported to the Presidential House.

In the blink of an opening and closing of gates, the police force had already cordoned off their target.

The divers continued singing in the middle of the street, with a line of cars at their backs, probably thinking that they had never had so much fun.

"We are unarmed. We want to speak with the President."

The police officer in uniform, with Mondolfo in the front demanding the President´s appearance, took his intercom and spoke in code. He was dictating numbers and it seemed to Mondolfo that he was reviewing his multiplication tables.

"The President is very busy. He asks you to return to your homes and he promises to go visit you as soon as he has time."

"Tell him, with all due respect, that we will not leave here, and that he must come speak to us."

The radio again, the codes again…

"Two and two are four, four, four and two are six, six and two are eight, and eight, sixteen. Over.

"Understood. Out."

As if enlightened by the Spirit of Rambo, it did not take the police much time to find the most effective way to get rid of that handful of foul-smelling skunks before their musky scent might impregnate forever the Presidential House. In a Jurassic manner, the tank with the water pump made its appearance: twenty-seven yards from its most elevated point. The divers' jaws dropped. They were petrified as they watched from a distance of nearly half a block how that antediluvian animal advanced toward them. They began to applaud because they thought that the President was coming from there. Behind the tank… the stalwart tanker truck.

The dinosaur raised its hose and ejaculated an exhilarating stream of cold water that left the divers soaked from head to foot… There were more shouts and cheering, and they applauded even louder. They were truly impressed by the manner in which the President was receiving them. They felt moved, privileged and they wanted to move closer.

The numbers man called out the lottery again, and a new discharge swept the poor people off the ground. At such a short distance the divers rolled on the ground and the shot of water left more than one diver gasping for air.

They were disconcerted. Única did not know what had become of Bacán until she found him sitting in the street crying. The stream of water had hit him forcefully.

Oso Carmuco was rolling about close by trying to free himself from the weight of his soaked cassock. His Bible shot out like a bullet and he never saw it again.

"Momboñombo, I don't like this. Look at what they did to our little boy…"

With his beard dripping the broth of several months without bathing, Mondolfo was trying to approach the police officers to explain to them that they were unarmed and that they only wanted to speak with don Junior María. But each time he attempted to approach, he would receive another discharge as a reply; finally the divers decided to take it all with good humor and began to dance around under the water.

Move on, move on. "With an A!" "Move on, move on." "With an E!" Mondolfo was running among them, shouting at them to stop… "With an I…" …to run away, because the police were already taking out their sticks… "With an O…" But for them the hose-bath was the most amusing thing they had ever seen in their lives, and there was no way to stop them… "With a U."

Única tried to calm down Bacán who was bawling because the stream of water had hit him in the chest and it was really hurting him.

Oso Carmuco was only able to get out of the cassock by ripping it to shreds through one of the holes that it possessed. The purple rag was thrown into the gutter and the current took it directly to the drain's mouth, which swallowed it in one bite.

There was no press, nor any witnesses other than the drivers who were jammed in the neighboring streets. Some people who were going by watched from a prudent distance but they said nothing.

The dance lasted until they reached the end of the water reserves in the tank's pump and in the tanker truck.

After shooting the last drop of water, the divers began to protest and to ask for more… As there was nothing more, they decided the party was over and took the road home around mid-afternoon, wet to the marrow of their bones.

The visit had been a failure, but only Mondolfo and Única saw it in that way.

Mondolfo was leaving defeated, straight to the garbage, like six months earlier. All the rest were going back happy, eager to play with the President again one day.

Bacán was going back with a terrible asthma attack.

They dried off on the road. The two hours it took them to return to the dump left them so tired that they did not even think about preparing anything for dinner. Everyone went directly to his or her cardboard bed.

* * *

"Our little boy won't stop coughing…"

Bacán was tossing and turning with fever, coughing and complaining.

"Única, we must do something. That boy is very sick. I have never seen him like this."

"He gets that way on me with the flu… and with that drenching they gave him…"

Against all the forecasts, the sun illuminated the shantytown the following day, and the divers came out to work as usual.

Oso Carmuco arrived early to Única's house and found a pitiful sight: neither Única nor Mondolfo had slept the entire night, and Bacán continued to tremble and cough no matter how much they warmed his chest and rubbed the nape of his neck with alcohol. The boy finally fell asleep as the morning warmed up. His parents took this moment to prepare breakfast. The three breakfasted on hot tortillas and black coffee because Oso Carmuco decided to stay to lend them his support.

"Doña Única, did you notice? I'm not a priest anymore…"

Stripped of his attributes of authority, Oso Carmuco assumed that he was relieved from his role, and in some ways, he felt that a weight had been lifted that had always exceeded his strength.

Única lamented not having been more responsible, not only for having attended the march, but even more so for not having prevented it.

Mondolfo only wanted to die like a dog; he could not stop blaming himself for the disaster.

"Let's take him to the hospital, Única. They have to attend to him there."

"He can't walk all the way there. Besides, he doesn't have any papers, and if they become aware of that, they will take him away from me…"

Mondolfo went out to the highway to try to convince someone to help him take his son to the hospital. An hour later he returned convinced that the world had turned to shit.

"Nobody wants to help us… If something happens to Bacán…"

"Don't say that! He will be fine very soon."

But he spent the morning coughing to the point of vomiting.

Several of the shantytown's children were in bed with the flu… "In bed" is an expression; they were lying down on their cardboard sweating fever.

"Who would have imagined all that water?" the other women divers would say to Única when they would come to see how Bacán was doing.

On the third day of the boy's illness, Mondolfo went out to search for a doctor.

"Somebody has to come to do something."

Hours later he returned shouting something that could be translated as the entire human species was scum, but he said it with other expressions of coarser language.

He did not get help.

"Our little boy doesn't want to eat anymore!"

Única was skin and bone. Mondolfo could not convince her to rest awhile, to sleep or to eat a little bit more of the stale bread that remained and something that the neighboring women had brought.

Their supplies were running out. Mondolfo would go out to dive for a while in the mornings. Their friends would help as much as they could. But by the middle of April Bacán's condition was irreversible. "Weakness," they would say; but it was more than that… it was pus in his lungs, it was greenish vomit, it was some twenty years of living in a trash dump.

Única would not leave her child's bed. She told him familiar stories…

"Once upon a time there was a very poor boy, very poor, and another boy who was very rich, very rich…"

She would sing the old familiar songs to him…

"When the moon is over the horizon, many dwarves play on the mountain…"

She would recite to him the familiar recitation "I grow a white rose…"

Mondolfo himself went to look for any doctor he could find in Río Azul and in San Francisco de Dos Ríos, but he did not find even a small boat in so much river, and the shipwreck seemed inevitable. When the doctors asked about the address and the old man told them, "up there, in the dump," they took it as a joke, or even worse, a trap.

Mondolfo returned home to find the same scenario: Bacán delirious with fever, singing songs, reciting, shouting … and Única petrified at his side. There was no longer any saint to whom she could promise even her own life if he or she would save her child, nor a rosary bead she had not worn out from running it between her fingers so much.

Oso Carmuco also did not move from the sickbed. Friends came and went, carrying and bringing the most unusual things that might bring relief to the boy; a toy, a pack of mint drops, rubbing alcohol, wood for the fire … Llorona, in an act that ended up breaking Única's spirit, detached the doll from her back, placed it next to Bacán and then went away to cry with as much bitterness as Única's. Everyone heard, each time nearer and nearer, the rumbling of the motor that never turns off; it was the garbage collector of death who had not passed by the dump for some time to collect the souls of refuse.

Única was bone thin; yellowish like a sculpture made

from a coffee root. Her clothes stuck to her body by the glue from her sweat and from the sweat of her son. In a couple of weeks she succeeded in personally verifying that it is not the faith of the poor that moves mountains. Her eyes darkened as if sinking into the quicksand of her incredulous expression, as if abandoning herself in a haze of demented resignation. She did not blink. She no longer had any tears or saliva.

Mondolfo would come and go from the shack, shouting with rage that it was not possible, or that all of it was his fault. He drank in one gulp the remains of some rum that Novio brought him in a cola bottle, but not even the burning in his throat could bring down the knot that was choking him.

And in the middle of the shipwreck of the human species, Bacán began to calm down little by little. The sounds of fighting cats coming from his chest made peace, and the boy died before his parents' empty stare.

Mondolfo cried like a hyena and clawed at his face, but Única was immobile, unaware of her husband's sobbing, of the sobbing of their friends.

"There's no justice, Única, by God, there's no justice…"

Mondolfo groaned between sobs.

"Yes, there is…" was the last thing she murmured, "but it's not done yet."

* * *

Some women divers shaved Bacán's face and they brightened it a little with blush. The entire night the community of divers kept vigil over the body, and a vigil was held also for Llorona's son, drowned in the trash and swallowed by the dump, since it hadn't been held at that time.

They laid one body next to the other, lifeless on the cot.

Some candles all around.

Weeping, praying and crying.

Strong coffee donated by everyone who had a little.

A calm night out at sea in the trash.

A recycled crucifix on the headboard.

A raggedy sun to begin the worst of days after the worst of nights.

With the first rays of light, Bacán's body was carried to the center of the dump and laid out directly on the ground. The body of Llorona's doll was resting on his chest.

Única ran her worn hand along her son's face. Llorona touched the doll's face. And everyone watched without surprise as the dump began to swallow them very slowly. The bodies were sinking softly between the earth and the trash as if in quicksand. Little by little they were being pulled under until only a lock of hair was in sight, for a few moments. And then they disappeared forever into the bowels of the dump.

It had all concluded when the tractor operators arrived and the first garbage trucks were forming in their straight lines.

Llorona was crying softly, without shouting or gasping for breath, and that was how she went down the hill, unnoticed, crying as she faded away along the edges of Río Azul. She never returned.

Única returned home guided by Mondolfo. In just two weeks they had grown years older. They walked with difficulty. She kept an impenetrable silence. He was crying on the inside.

Their days ran together rapidly, undifferentiated, identical and interminable. Única would only drink a teaspoonful of sugar water that Mondolfo would give her.

"Don't you die on me too, old woman."

He did not read a newspaper again the rest of his life. He never found out that the Río Azul community had extended the deadline agreed to with the Government to give the new dump in Esparza more time.

Eat a little, look it's mashed taro root.

Nor did he realize either that Esparza's dump would never be built.

He did not know that the University had carried out a real study on the environmental impact in which it was demonstrated that the land in Cabezas de Esparza was not the wasteland that the Government was saying, but rather the absolute contrary. It was the key point where the shallow marine waters of the Mero estuary met the subterranean waters, and the point where the drainage system from the Barbudal mountain stream was collected.

"Say something to me, my old woman, anything at all… tell me that I was to blame…"

However, nothing mattered any longer to Mondolfo, if the government was closing the dump or if God was closing the universe.

Their supplies depleted, Mondolfo went back to diving. He would dive rabidly the entire morning and he would return home to find Única immersed in her shell. Then he would speak to her, telling her about his morning at work, the anecdotes, the successes from his diving…no response, not even a glance on which to hang a slim hope.

"You saved me Única, and now you won't let me save you. It was all a lie…" Mondolfo would protest far from understanding that he could complain about anything to her except the lie that she had built day by day throughout twenty years or more. Because that had been her masterpiece, bringing with her to the dump familial traditions, good manners, a schedule for meals, and Good Friday's rosary.

"By God, what insanity!"

Cooking scraps over a fire to feed a great many poor people who would contribute almost nothing more than their hunger's curse.

"What insanity, damn it all!"

Celebrating the fifteenth of September as if in poverty enslavement and independence could be distinguished.

But the entire Creation of Única's World, on that Seventh Day of that second week had crumbled to its very foundations.

Mondolfo spoke to her between chokes and a raspy crying that agitated his asthma; he spoke with his entire life story stuck in his throat. While Única, like a rag doll, was breathing through force of habit, suspended in her absurdity.

The door opened with a shove. The light blinded Mondolfo's pupils. It was don Retana who had dragged his eighty-five years to Única's shack, his horrific arthritis and his sadness at not having found out about the tragedy until then. The elderly man came in silently, he went up to Única, looked at her in silence, and for a long time silently caressed her face and her loose hair. And he saw on the ground the clipped marionette strings with which she had attached herself to life all those years.

The elderly man sat down in silence at Mondolfo's side and lent him the only thing that all in all, a human being can lend to another: his broken-down shoulder. There, Mondolfo finished crying what remained of his reservoirs of pain.

* * *

Mondolfo Moya Garro decided that their days at the dump were finished. He put together his family's savings, brought his friends together and announced that they were leaving there.

The ones closest to them contributed something to the old people's cause, and Oso Carmuco emptied the chests of his former ministry into Mondolfo's hands.

They left the shack to don Retana. The cot would afford him very soon a more dignified death than the cardboard on the ground.

Mondolfo packed some things convinced that rather than being of use to them, they would get in their way, but he did not have the heart to get rid of Bacán's favorite book, nor one or another of his toys. He packed a round hotplate for cooking tortillas, a large pot, some threadbare blankets, and the very few personal articles of clothing that they had.

Oso Carmuco accompanied them to the Puntarenas bus station, he embraced them tightly, he kissed Única and he told her choking up that she had been his mother too. And he danced the giant's dance along the sidewalk to make Mondolfo laugh. He smiled and waved goodbye with his hand. Oso Carmuco went away dancing like a bear and he disappeared forever down the street.

A long line… glares of disgust and distrust.

"Get out of the line, please…"

"But we're going to Puntarenas!"

"You don't say! And what hotel are you going to?"

Laughter from the people… glares of disgust and distrust…

"Get out of the line, please, before I call the police."

The word "police" provoked a shiver in Única's decimated body. Mondolfo experienced the miracle of rage evaporating from his eyes, and in one last prudent act, he swallowed what he was going to spit into the face of the man from behind the ticket window, who had bothered to abandon his post in order to throw them out of the line. He put his arm around Única and they moved away.

The old people began to retrace their steps with the slowness of sure knowledge that they no longer had any place in this world, or in all probability, in the other.

They walked from Puntarenas station to Parque de la Merced and they sat down on a bench with a view of Second Avenue.

"We have arrived, my dear old woman! Do you like Puntarenas?"

Mondolfo made his wife as comfortable as he could on the concrete bench. He sat down at her side, put their things underneath, directly onto the ground, and they devoted themselves completely to contemplating the sea.

"You like the sound of the sea, Única!"

Her expression did not move from where it was. He took her face with his hand and pointed her eyes toward the sea, but the sea seemed small … it did not match the size of their pain.

"Look at the little boats, look how they sway!"

It was noon. They did not have lunch, nor did they move from where they had run aground. Neither did they have dinner. He managed to get her to drink a few sips of sugar water that he had brought in a bottle. Afterwards he drank and saved some for later.

Already growing dark, they wrapped themselves in their burlap sacks and the evening came upon them without their noticing it. Única had closed her eyes for the first time in several days, and he felt relief.

Between the sounds of exhaust, the sea's motors on Second Avenue and exhaustion, the old people slept.

Early, almost at dawn, Mondolfo awoke with his usual start. Única had already opened her eyes, but she showed no signs of having slept or of having stayed awake, or anything.

Mondolfo picked up the burlap sacks; he placed the bundle at her side and left to find something to eat for breakfast. He returned a little while later with some rolls spread with jelly. Única was still immovable in her shell.

He was able to get her to swallow a roll, virtually crumb by crumb. There was no coffee that morning, nor ever again.

The sea was roiling as if moved by invisible tractors. Against the light, the seagulls looked black. The asphalt beach appeared to be sand in Mondolfo's useless description. The people between the waves of cars reminded him of his friends. The air was fresher than in the dump, but that was something he would no longer notice ever again.

Their savings would suffice at the most for one week of bread with jelly.

It took three days of looking at the sea for Mondolfo to be convinced that their situation would not change. However, on the morning of the fourth day, the old man managed to steal a rose from a stall in the Central Market.

After a shantytown breakfast, he put the rose into Única's hands, he took her to the edge of the gutter and showed her how to pull the petals off slowly, and to throw the petals one by one into the waves, one by one, without throwing another until the previous one had disappeared; stripping it completely down to the bud, and then tossing it away with its stalk and watching it move away floating, until also disappearing into the jaws of the drain.

After the ritual... back to the bench to look at the sea.

Their funds depleted, Mondolfo saw that it was time to work again in the last job he had learned in his life. He did the best he could to make Única comfortable; he took a cloth bag and began to go up and down the concrete beaches, to dive in the market's surrounding areas and along the streets...

At the end of the day's work he returned with the

bag filled.

"The world is full of trash."

Living as a diver on firm ground was not a problem. The real tragedy was watching Única wrapped in her shell of sorrow, absent, oblivious to all movement around her. She would only get up from her place early every morning for the ritual of pulling the petals from the rose, the same rose each day for her, but always stolen from different flower shops.

The minuscule gutter-sea would accept the sacrifice and gulp down the petals as if swallowing suffering, certain to digest it, as the ancient sea had done always from the moment humanity had invented pain. Mondolfo trusted that the waves would bring Única back to him, would restore her cellophane soul, and would put back into her eyes an effort to look, which was why he never stopped talking and talking about the sea foam, about the ships, about the fishermen and about the sunsets.

"Look, what a line of pelicans, Única, over there, between the palm trees! Look at the people swimming!"

On the eastern coast the Cathedral de la Merced looked like a shipwreck. On the western coast, San Juan de Dios Hospital looked like a fishing boat...

The sea fit entirely into Mondolfo Moya Garro's mouth, and he emptied it entirely into Única's ear...

"Those over there are seagulls, my sweet old girl..." and he would point with his trembling hand at the

Castilla's doves that inundated the park.

The landscape had devoured them. Once accommodated on their concrete bench, they had become invisible between the smoke from the exhaust, the merciless horns, and the rest of the park's community, where a couple of indigent elderly neither added to anything nor took away from anything.

"What are we going to do when the rains return?"

High tide was from six o'clock in the morning until around nine o'clock, rush hour, hundreds of cars, thousands of people in all directions.

Low tide was around mid-morning. Every kind of casual transaction was carried out throughout the park's pathways. Once in a while a pair of police officers would pass in front of the old people and they would look at them from out of the corner of their eyes. Mondolfo would get agitated; Única was no longer capable of perceiving her surroundings.

Mondolfo was diving along the nearby streets, talking to himself, crossing from one sidewalk to the opposite side, getting in the way of cars, entering stores from where he was chased immediately, asking for credit along the stretch of peddlers, where from time to time he would get a piece of fruit past its prime, or he would pick one up from the street... In essence, he was earning sustenance for him and for his companion, but without the questions or the previous angst... Why? What for? And all those existential indulgences that he had allowed himself when he was poor, when he was living under a roof at the dump.

"What a smell of fish, Única!"

They would run him out of the flower shops with shouts and threats. So he began to pick up any flower he could find in the trash along the stretch of the marketplace. He would do it because he had become accustomed to doing it, nothing more; and not because he hoped that by throwing petals against the gutter's waves a hint of something close to a smile might cross Única's face... something that might look like one and not Mondolfo's empty happiness when he would see it and would swear to having seen a glimpse of life in her face, a fleeting spark that left no trail, that would disappear, that would leave her like a vague cloud from the beach of her false teeth.

DIÁLOGOS